A PRIVATE MOON

PETER BENSON

ALMA BOOKS

ALMA BOOKS LTD
London House
243–253 Lower Mortlake Road
Richmond
Surrey TW9 2LL
United Kingdom
www.almabooks.com

First published by Hodder and Stoughton in 1995
This edition published by Alma Books Limited in 2012
Copyright © Peter Benson, 1995

Peter Benson asserts his moral right to be identified as the author of
this work in accordance with the Copyright, Designs and Patents Act
1988

Printed and bound by CPI Group (UK) Ltd, Croydon, CR0 4YY

Typeset by Tetragon

ISBN: 978-1-84688-196-1

The thief
left it behind –
the moon at the window.

Ryokan

1

Brighton's houses stood like stones in fields of snow. Its streets were quiet, its lights shone in a dull light, and the sea washed its lonely shore. The Palace Pier creaked. The Pavilion froze. Gardens dreamed. Clocks stopped. An aeroplane droned overhead, and a ship hooted through a distant fog-bank.

Frank sat in his car and stared at a house. The client's wife was inside, lying in bed with a woman.

Frank yawned and scratched his chin. The car smelt of cold coffee and snow.

He turned on the radio. A Christmas carol was playing, and then a woman began to talk about the importance of planning. Frank turned the radio off.

He looked at the house again, and the upstairs window on the left. The curtains were drawn, it was half-past two in the afternoon. The first two weeks of December had been warm, but now it was cold. Grit covered the roads and pavements, and the sky hung low. A man with a dog walked by; a cat on a wall crouched to watch them pass, then jumped down and disappeared into a garden. Frank rested his head in the palm of his left hand, and closed his eyes.

His mobile rang.

'Frank?'

'Bob.' Bob sat with his feet on his office desk, swopped the receiver from his right hand to his left.

'You at Austin's place?'

'Yes.'

'Any change?'

'No...'

'Then come in. We've got another job.'

'Now?'

'Now, Frank,' and Bob hung up.

Frank held the phone in his hand for a moment, then put it down. He took one last look at the house, then drove back to the office.

Bob was standing at the window with his hands behind his back, staring down at the street. He'd watched Frank park, he'd watched him sit in the car for a minute and he'd watched him smooth his hair down as he walked to the office. He'd heard his feet on the stairs, and a clatter as he opened the outer door.

Frank ambled into the office, hung his coat on the back of the door and sat down. His legs were too big for his body and the chair he sat in; he had never learnt what to do with them. One minute they stretched out straight, and then they were tucked under him like bags of rubbish. Or he crossed them, and the one on top swung like a clockwork part. Now, he had them out straight. 'So,' he said. 'What's the new job?'

Bob stared out of the window until a pair of shopping women had passed by, then bent down, picked a bottle of whisky off the floor and put it on the desk. 'This,' he said.

Frank bent his left leg up, picked at a loose cotton, looked at his watch and said, 'It's three o'clock.'

'Where's your sense of adventure?'

Frank looked at his oldest friend and shook his head. 'Adventure?' he said.

'Sure,' said Bob.

'If I want adventure, I phone Austin and tell him his wife's in bed with his sister.'

'No kidding.'

Frank looked at the bottle, looked at Bob and then back at the bottle. It was full. A police car wailed beneath the window, and grey snow began to fall. The smell of burnt milk hung in the air. Bob shook his head and said, 'It's not meant to be this way.' He opened a desk drawer and took out two glasses. He took the phone off the hook, unscrewed the bottle and kicked off his shoes.

* * *

At half-past nine, as the lightest shower of snow drifted in the air, Frank let himself into Mrs Platt's house, stamped his feet on the mat, checked the hall table for post and began to climb the stairs. He had his left foot on the third step when Mrs Platt put her head around her door and said, 'Long day, Frank?' He heard her caged-bird cheep, leaned towards her and nodded. 'Yes.'

Mrs Platt was a small woman with a stoop and pale, milky eyes. Her cheeks, chin, forehead and neck were criss-crossed with deep lines. Her skin looked as though it had been peeled from a pale tree and stuck on to her bones with imperfect glue. She had been a landlady for thirty years, a widow for ten, and had owned many budgies. She was seventy-seven, and had seen King Edward VIII sitting in a car at traffic lights in Brighton. His vacuous gaze and the classical set of his jaw had stunned her; at the time she'd sensed that he was heading for tragedy, but she'd told no one. She used eau-de-Cologne, and always wore something black. She lived on the bottom floor of her house, in four rooms. She often gave the impression of not being there, of being at odds with the world, but she knew who she was, where she was, and who lived in her house. Since Mr Platt had died, she had lived quietly, she didn't impose herself on her tenants, and she ate simply. She avoided eggs but liked fresh vegetables. In the old days, she had kept an allotment, but she couldn't dig any more. Now she bought her sprouts, purple sprouting, cabbage and carrots from a shop. She was a trusting woman, and watched *Home and Away* and *Neighbours* every day. She wore glasses to read, and had been abroad once. She had visited Calais in 1965, a treat Mr Platt had arranged. He had bought her a souvenir of the town, a sea-shell she kept on her mantelpiece next to a postcard of Brighton in the old days.

'It's been a long day,' said Frank.

'You work too hard,' she said.

'I work too hard,' he said. 'Yes.'

'You should have a holiday.'

Frank felt this idea dive into his head and thrash about. It churned up memories, fears and worry. 'What?' he said.

'A holiday,' said Mrs Platt. 'We used to go to Whitby.'

'Whitby?' said Frank.

'Oh yes. Every year. It's lovely there.'

The bird stopped cheeping, and Mrs Platt edged back into her room and closed the door without another word. Frank stood on the third step for half a minute as the idea of a holiday began to fail and then drown; then he climbed to the first landing, leant on the banister and stared at Lisa's door.

Strings of light bled from its edges, and the sound of a television. Frank had lived above her for three years. She worked in a chemist's, collected teapots and had a boyfriend called Adrian. She would come up and talk. She had a sharp nose, and had holidayed in six Mediterranean countries. She had perfect fingernails, and the ghosts of freckles covered her face. Frank looked at his own fingernails, then climbed the stairs to the second floor. He let himself in, took a bottle of Volvic from the fridge and pulled a chair to the window. He sat down, put his feet on the sill and stared at the winter.

Half an hour later, there was a knock on the door. The snow had stopped and settled, and now threads of fog were gathering around the streetlights. A car slewed up the street below, and a cold dog barked. The knock dropped into his mind like a stone in a still lake; he knew what it was, but as the ripples of sound began to spread out, he began to forget. A knock or someone dropping a saucepan downstairs? It came again. He stood up and opened the door. It was Lisa. She smiled and said, 'Hey, Frank! Don't answer it if you don't want to.' She flicked her right hand at her hair.

'I'm sorry,' he mumbled.

'Sorry!' She patted his arm and laughed.

'Come in,' he said.

'Thanks.' She took two steps, and stood in the middle of Frank's room.

It was tidy. There was a carefully made bed against one wall, and a typewriter on a table against the other. There was a stack of plain paper next to the typewriter, and a mug of pens. The window was opposite the door. A screened alcove hid a sink, draining-board, fridge and cooker, and a neat row of knives attached to a magnetic strip. Cups and saucers were washed, dried and stacked in glass-fronted cupboards. A door at the foot of the bed led to a tiny bathroom. Frank had shelves of books and a small collection of records, mainly classical favourites. The room had a fresh smell, it was dusted and vacuumed. It was homely but antiseptic, a particular type of man's room. There was a picture of a mountain lake over the table, and a map of the world over the bed. There were pins stuck in the map, but Lisa had never asked Frank what the pins meant. She sat in an easy chair by the window, he slumped in his, crossed his legs and she said, 'Got anything to drink?'

He held up the Volvic.

'Water?' she said.

'Sorry,' he said.

'Again?' she said, and she pulled a bottle of Scotch out of her pocket. 'Come on, I've got news for you.'

'News?'

'You bet. Want to try and guess?'

'Guess?'

She put the bottle on the floor and ran her fingers through her hair. 'Are you going to repeat every last word I say?'

'No,' he said, and he rubbed his forehead. 'I'm…'

'Careful…'

Frank pointed. 'Bob made me drink half a bottle of that this afternoon; I don't know.'

'Please,' she said, and she tapped his knee. 'We're celebrating!'

'What?'

'You've got to guess!'

'Oh yes,' said Frank. 'A guessing game. I don't like them. Guessing's gambling dressed like a kid; no.' He shook his head, and uncrossed his legs. He tried to tuck them to the left, then to the right, then crossed them again. 'You tell me, Lisa. What are we celebrating?'

'Frank; how long have we known each other?'

'Three years last October.'

'And we're friends, right?'

'I hope so.' Bob's whisky had stalled Frank's head and rearranged fuses; now Lisa banged the fuses back, and the shadows on her face froze his haze. He sat up, repeated, 'I hope so,' and added, 'Of course we're friends.'

'Good.'

'Why?' Frank was sober now and he was on the case. He smelt trouble and he tasted worry, and all the honed edges of his work stood up. 'Lisa?'

'No,' she said, and she hid her mouth behind her hand. 'No trouble,' she said, and she smiled a smile that stretched from water to whisky. 'I'm pregnant.'

Frank had been around. He'd met a man who'd filled a surfboard with dope and left it on a train, and he'd met children who'd sneaked into a zoo and stolen a penguin. He'd spent ten years working through continental Europe, and had seen a small Italian woman knock out an enormous German with one punch, and he'd watched a French woman climb a thousand feet of sheer rock with only suntan oil for protection. He'd seen Albanian children fighting over a crushed Coke tin, and he'd watched dozens of Irishmen fall asleep on a cold beach. He was fifty-two; he had worked for a firm that fitted special floors in hospitals, and he had worked as an orderly in a home for children with cerebral palsy. He had slept with two women. He could play the mouth organ. He had raked the gravel in the Tuileries, and sorted fish in Ostend. He was not malicious, deceitful or dangerous. He had expressive hands and used them when he talked. He liked people, but he could not sustain a relationship. He was neat, he hated mess. He didn't abuse his body, and did not enjoy eating in restaurants. He had grey hair, and had worked for Bob, an old friend from the army, for twelve years. He enjoyed cooking fish and used to collect stamps. He'd never married, and he had never been to Australia. He'd seen a man shoot another man in Rome and walk out of the restaurant whistling. He'd seen Frank Sinatra carrying a Duty Free bag through Frankfurt airport, and watched a three-legged dog race in Wales, but he'd never spent more than twenty minutes with a pregnant woman.

'Pregnant?' he said.

Lisa nodded, smiled, picked up the bottle and her eyes began to crease. 'Yes.'

'And it's, it's…' Frank struggled to find the word. It was there, but it wasn't. There was something you said, a key, and with it a pregnant woman knew she could trust you. He uncrossed his legs, bundled them under the chair and said, 'It's…' again.

'Time you got some glasses?'

'Yes,' he said, and he put out his hand to Lisa as he stood up. 'You're okay?'

'Fine.'

'Good,' he said, and his inadequacy boiled into his head. He took two glasses from a cupboard, fetched a tea-cloth and wiped them; as he held one up to the light, he said, 'When's it due?'

'July.'

'And Adrian, he's…'

'Oh yeah.' She picked up the bottle and Frank held out a glass. 'He's over the moon,' she said. Adrian loved her, and she loved him. She poured the whisky, and Frank sat down again. He looked at his legs and decided to leave them as they were, sticking out in a friendly way. 'He can't wait,' she said, and she took a drink, and rubbed her lips with the side of her forefinger. 'But father…'

Frank knew about Lisa's father. The man had throttled her greyhound to death with a parsnip.

'Have you told him?'

'Not yet.'

'What's he going to say?'

Lisa shrugged. 'Good question.'

11

Lisa's father was in Maidstone gaol, locked up for five years for burglary, his third offence.

'Answer?' Frank swilled his whisky around the glass and took a sip.

'I'm going to write to him; it'll be all right. He can't get to me.'

'That bad?'

'That bad,' said Lisa, and she poured some more whisky. 'But I don't care.' She looked at Frank. 'How old are you?'

'Fifty-one… two.'

'You could be him,' she said.

'No I couldn't,' he said, and as she stared at him but didn't say anything else, he glanced out of the window. The snow was falling again, and the lights of the city cast a dome of orange light into the night that hung like a caul. The sound of slow-moving traffic drifted to where they sat, high in Mrs Platt's house in the third week of December.

2

In the morning, Frank sat in Bob's office and waited. The phone rang but he didn't answer it. The phone wasn't his responsibility.

He looked at his watch. It was half-past ten. He sipped a cup of coffee and thought about Lisa and her father. How does having children change a man, and how could a man think a child was his property? Was a daughter yours, or a small person who's come to stay for a while? Would a child make me feel important, or inadequate? When you're pregnant, can you feel the child feeding off you? Would Lisa and Adrian let him take the baby for a walk? Frank ran his fingers around the rim of his coffee cup, and coughed.

He had one memory of his father, a faded image of a smiling khaki figure standing against a blue sky holding a fishing rod. There was sea in the memory, and tall cliffs. The sea was calm and the weather was warm. There were seagulls in the sky, and vapour trails. It was 1945, Frank was four, and his father was going away to die in Germany. He had a moustache and smelt of carbolic, and he kissed Frank's mother on the lips. Frank could take this memory and examine its detail, but he controlled himself. Once he had felt betrayed by his father's death, and later, as he watched his mother struggle to hold on, he had despaired; now he was dispassionate. Life was a mistake that happened. Do people favours, give yourself a present every week and don't be the first to raise your voice. A mistake can be corrected. You come alone, you go alone, you are alone. Tell no one anything and eat fish. Feed your brain, read a lot and go for one long walk a week. Enjoy your work.

Frank enjoyed his. He liked helping people. Matrimonial, bona fides, surveillance, proof of evidence, missing persons, insurance investigation; all these words were bells to him. When Bob had asked him to bring his experience to Brighton and work for the agency, he had known. There had been no break between the desire and the possibility; the sun had been shining, and Bob had smiled. Bob had stopped smiling seven years later, for no reason he wanted to explain. Now it was snowing, and the phone in the office stopped ringing; Frank took the receiver off the hook and laid it on its side. It buzzed at the desk for half a minute, then stopped. The silence was light and drifted in the air.

Bob sat in his car and looked up at the office. He was smoking a cigarette, but didn't want to. He was tired but he had a dream, his heart's construction, and this kept him awake. It had kept him awake for a year, but he didn't mind. He played with it, tweaked its edges and gently rearranged its clothes. He wanted to give up the agency and put his past behind him. He was divorced, had three children he hadn't seen for five years and owed the bank sixty thousand pounds. He had pains in his back that shot into his neck, and he coughed for five minutes every morning. He wanted to get healthy, to flush his body and feel his cheeks burn. He thought about soap and water, and all the different ways you could clean your body. He wanted to be able to spend a whole day feeding ducks, or on the beach, and a whole night asleep. He wanted to be able to spend two hours over a meal, and he wanted to watch television programmes that started at half-eight in the morning. Now, he flicked his cigarette into the gutter, said, 'Shit!' to himself, and then, 'No.' He rubbed his eyes, climbed out of the car, slammed the door and crossed the road.

When he reached the pavement, he put his left foot on a plate of ice, held his balance for a moment and then fell over.

First, he hit his knee; he put his hand out, tried to break the fall, but the hand hit more ice and he went down on his head. He cracked himself above the right eye, and a pavement edge cut him. He bled easily; within seconds, blood was blinding him. He flayed his arms, struggled up and staggered to the office door. A woman pushing a baby in a pram stopped to watch him cross in front of her, and a man with a plastic bag turned and shook his head. The sky was full of the yellow darkness that feeds snow; Bob took a handkerchief from his pocket, mopped his face and climbed the stairs to the office. He saw Frank waiting for him, he felt hot and then he felt cold. He dreamed of a world where telephones didn't ring, and he wanted a world of wild salmon. Life was a mistake but you had to live it by degrees; 'Frank,' he said.

'What happened to you?' said Frank.

Snow in winter. The Innuit have a hundred words for 'snow' and one word for 'tree'. The English have one word for 'snow' and a thousand words for 'tree'. The sky began to belch over Bob and Frank's office; as Bob washed his cut in a small sink, he thought about Innuit squatting over holes in the ice, and he thought about how fish can smell bait from miles away, through freezing salt water. He tasted his blood and thought how natural it was. He thought about Frank and wondered how he was. Frank lived alone, Frank had no family, Frank cooked fish and drank water, and listened to classical favourites. Frank never said anything about his private life. Frank was an island. I am an island, thought Bob, but I have a well on my west coast. Frank has to rely on rain-water. He has to remember to put buckets out before he goes to bed. He has to catch his life, but mine is bubbling up around my feet. All I have to do is bend down and drink. Bob turned off the taps, shook his hands dry and stood up and dabbed at his face with a towel. 'Yes,' he said.

'Yes?' said Frank.

'Yes.'

'You okay?'

'Yes.'

'No,' said Frank. 'Are you going to be all right?'

'Yes,' said Bob. 'I've never been better.'

Frank laughed at his friend and Bob laughed back; Frank stood up and Bob sat in his chair.

Outside, the sky opened and it began to snow; big flakes drifted past the office window like breath. A silence floated over the town with the flakes; conversation came hushed, no doors slammed and car tyres rolled with whispers. 'Okay,' said Frank, and the word was a note. 'What do you want me to do?'

Bob put the tips of his fingers together, spread them, flexed them, leant back, stared at the ceiling and said, 'Tell her.'

'Tell who?'

'Austin's wife.'

Frank looked at his nails. 'His wife?'

'Tell her...' said Bob, 'we've been following her for the last two weeks. That we know everything.' He put a finger to his cut. It was nothing. 'Give her a break.'

'Are you serious?' Frank looked at his friend, and his friend looked back with fat blue eyes.

'Absolutely.'

'Okay.' Frank looked at his shoes, noticed a speck on one and bent to rub it off. When he sat up again, he said, 'And then what? Go round and give him the bill?'

'And this.' He pushed a case report across the desk. 'It's all in there.'

Frank snorted. 'And tell him what?'

'That his wife's been studying Tai Chi with his sister.'

Now Frank laughed. 'Tai Chi?'

'Yes. It's a Chinese exercise…'

'I know what it is.'

'… and meditation. It's supposed to prolong active life…'

'Where? Where's she supposed to be doing this?'

'Places, dates, times.' Bob tapped the report and then said, 'Before you see her, buy a book about it, then go round to her place and give it to her. Explain why, and where you come from, and let her read the report. She can make notes.'

Frank sat back and rubbed his forehead. He studied Bob's face, and watched the man's eyes swivel from left to right. There was an unusual smile on his face, something that bothered Frank; it wasn't a smile of pleasure, relief or contentment, there was something odd behind it. 'She'll love me for it?'

'We're doing her a favour.' Bob put his hand over his heart and took a deep breath. His smile dropped, and he winced.

'Are you okay?'

Bob nodded.

'You ought to see someone about that knock.' Frank pointed at his friend's head and at the purpling wound.

'Don't worry about me; you worry about Austin.' Bob picked up a sealed envelope from the desk and passed it to Frank. 'This is his bill. Don't forget to tell him—'

'Ten per cent discount for early settlement.'

'You got it.'

3

Lisa was twenty, and had been born in Brighton. When she was six, she wanted to be a pop singer, when she was seven, she wanted to be the woman who swung the letters on *Wheel of Fortune*, and when she was eight, she wanted to work on the Palace Pier with Madame Chin, a fortune-teller. For her ninth birthday, her father robbed a toyshop and gave her a magic set; he was arrested during her party. Her friends thought the chase through the house, the policemen falling over the fence at the bottom of the garden, and the howls of pain as her father was pinned against a side wall and given a good kicking, were part of the entertainment. The magic set was taken away as evidence.

When she was ten, her ambitions took a swing; she decided to join the army. She began to imagine herself as the brother she didn't have, she built a secret camp in a park, and laid ambushes for old men with dogs. She got posters of tanks and soldiers skiing in Norway and stuck them on her bedroom wall. She dreamed in khaki and taught herself Morse code. When her mother told her that women couldn't be soldiers, she refused to listen, she refused to allow her goal to be subverted. She strengthened her resolve, she learnt to identify every cap-badge in the British army, and watched every war movie she could.

Then, suddenly, she changed. At fourteen, she turned vegetarian, ripped down her tank posters and met a boy called Robin. She lost interest in ambition, left school at sixteen and moved in with him. She signed on, got up late, smoked dope and never went to bed before three o'clock in the morning. She lived like this for two years; then her mother died, and the shock readjusted her head. She left Robin and found the flat in Mrs Platt's house, and decided to work her grief away. She got a job stacking supermarket shelves, then moved on to the chemist's. She washed her hair every day, and met Adrian. Now she was dreaming of family life, a bigger flat and an enormous bed. During her lunch-break, she sat down and wrote a letter to her father. She didn't explain anything; she just told him what had happened and how happy she was. She had always wanted a child, did he remember that? Did he remember when she used to keep rabbits and pretend that they were her family? Now she didn't have to pretend any more. She wrote that one day Adrian was going to own his own garage, and that he loved her. She wrote that she wasn't going to visit Maidstone until the baby was born; she had been feeling sick in the mornings and didn't want to risk upsetting herself. She wrote that she hoped this was all right, that it was understood. She wrote that she'd write again, and then went back to work.

She was advising an old man on a choice of nail-clippers as Frank drove past the shop. He slowed to see if he could see her, but advertisements for photograph developing and pain-killers covered the window; he accelerated up Wheel Road, waited for the lights to change at the top junction, swung left, then right, then right again, and cruised into Spender Avenue. He parked and walked to the bookshop.

He liked bookshops but they made him feel uncomfortable. He didn't want to be sucked into a conversation with a stranger about something he didn't know. Knowledge bred wisdom or chaos, mainly chaos, he thought. He read history books, sometimes biographies. Events that were over and people that were dead; these were safe areas. Now he tried to look at ease; he put one hand in his pocket, then another, then both at once, then took them both out and let them swing. He narrowly avoided upsetting a display with his feet, and a sales assistant asked him if he needed any help, but he shook his head. He would find what he wanted, and when he had, he would buy it. He was a big man in a big shop, and Tai Chi was a big subject. China was a big country, and there are at least a billion Chinese people in the world.

He passed shelves of guidebooks to foreign places, ran his fingers along some teach-yourself language books, turned a corner and reached the Pregnancy and Motherhood section. He spotted a sign that read 'Self-Improvement' but was stopped by a display of Dr Miriam Stoppard's *New Pregnancy and Birth Book*. He picked one up, opened it and read page 132. 'Sports Activities'. There was a picture of a pregnant woman swimming; Dr Stoppard wrote that she went swimming two weeks before the birth of her second baby. Frank was amazed. He flipped the pages back and looked at pages of pictures of embryos developing in the womb; he was reminded of something he had dreamt, and was slapped by his own ignorance.

He thought about the things Lisa would have to go through, and decided that he should know what to expect. He tucked a copy under his arm, took a step back and bumped into a pregnant woman.

'Oh God,' he said, and he dropped the book, 'I'm sorry.'

'Don't worry,' said the woman.

'Are you sure? I mean…'

'Really.' The woman took a deep breath and put her hand on her belly. 'We're fine.'

Frank looked around for someone else. 'Sorry?' he said.

'Don't be,' said the woman, and, 'You dropped your book.'

'Oh yes.' He looked at the floor and bent to pick it up; he glanced at the cover and felt a peculiar sensation creep into his cheeks. It was hot, and it affected his eyes. He squinted, and the woman said, 'What's the matter?'

'Nothing.'

She smiled. 'You're blushing.'

'What?'

'You're blushing.'

Frank was amazed. Strange things were happening to him. He said sorry again and hurried away to find a book about Tai Chi.

Tai Chi is an interesting subject; Frank read some of *Tai Chi: A Guide to the 48 Step Form* while he drank a cup of coffee at Juliet's Coffee and Video Bar. He sat at a corner table facing the door, the window, the counter and the racks of videos for rent. He was alone; Juliet was out the back, washing breakfast dishes, whistling to herself. The place smelt of slush and stale doughnuts, condensation streamed down the window, a television showed a thriller with the sound down. A man was chased up a dark street, a car skidded to a halt, a gun fired two shots. A man's face was seen in close-up, blood streaming from a wound to his cheek; Frank put the book down, stared at the screen and thought about Bob. Bob was the brains and the organisation, Frank was the charming muscle and the man who sat in cars for hours. Frank had tried to plan and organise, but his mind got in the way. There was something about telephones that split his brain; he had never kept a diary, and he didn't own a calendar. He hated numbers and he hated loose change. Reading about Tai Chi had given him something to think about. In ancient China, peasant children would be killed so their mothers could breast-feed the Imperial Pekinese dogs. He remembered reading this once, but he couldn't recall where, or when. He left Juliet a tip, and went to see Mrs Austin.

Mrs Platt poked a fresh cuttlefish through the bars of Joey's cage, but Joey didn't move. He huddled by a maize stick with one eye open and the other closed. One of his toes poked out, and he held his mouth open; he had some primeval memory in his head, and it was bothering him. There was a cliff, there was a huge sky and red earth, there were trees in leaf and there were thousands of other budgies chirping. The noise was deafening; Joey closed the other eye as his head filled with sound. He felt himself take off and fly over a deep ravine. He saw a river below him, a huge flock of sheep and a man on horseback, but when he opened his eye again, all he saw was Mrs Platt, a cuttlefish and the roses on the wallpaper of her flat. Joey closed his eye again, Mrs Platt shook her head, ran her fingers down the bars of the bird's cage, sighed and went to make a fresh pot of tea.

As she stood over her kettle, she worked out that she'd had Joey ten years. She remembered the shop where she had bought him, and how the woman behind the counter had been so helpful. Since then, the bird had never pined, showed signs of boredom, gone off its food or fallen off its perch. It had been a perfect companion, and now it was dying. Oh, life is a bastard and then we die. Religions were designed by the imaginative for the unimaginative to consider theirs; God is not dead, how could something that never existed die? Mrs Platt knew that religion was a comfort, and she understood why people needed it to fill some hole in their minds, but she also understood the con. Even something as simple as Joey understood the con, and that comforted her. With his one eye open and the other closed, he was not stupid. Mrs Platt decided to call the vet.

Frank drove slowly to Mr Austin's sister's house, where Mrs Austin was standing with her arms around the woman. The book about Tai Chi lay on the passenger seat, the roads were gritted and pedestrians walked carefully. The sun was hidden by cloud.

Frank worried. Bob had never asked him to work like this. He had never asked him to deceive a client. The client was always right, the client paid their wages. You gave him the information he was paying for and you moved on to the next case. Subjectivity wasn't in it; it was a dispassionate world, and all living things, when faced with primeval dreams, knew it. The risks of the work did not worry Frank, but he was made nervous by unexpected twists. He was forced to ask questions he hadn't expected; why was Bob trying to protect Mrs Austin? Or was he trying to protect Miss Austin? Or was the Austin case a diversion? Was Bob losing it? Frank turned into Gordon Road and parked as the lighest shower of snow fell, then stopped.

He stood in front of Miss Austin's front door and rang the bell. He held the Tai Chi book under his arm and took deep breaths. A minute passed; he rang again, and the door was opened immediately by a thin woman in a dressing-gown. He recognised her as Miss Austin; he lowered his eyes, and in a soft, unalarming voice, said, 'Miss Austin? My name is Frank, and I've got a message from your brother.'

'Cyril?' she said. 'Is something wrong?'

'Yes...' said Frank, 'and no.'

Miss Austin held the collar of her dressing-gown, took a step back and said, 'You'd better come in.'

'Thanks.'

Frank knew every inch of the outside of the house he was now standing in; it was strange to him to be in it. There was a smell of perfume in the hall, and the sound of movement upstairs; he was led to the kitchen, where Miss Austin filled a kettle with water and said, 'Please.' She pointed to a chair. 'Sit down. Would you like a cup of tea?'

'Thanks.'

She fetched a pot from a cupboard and began to fiddle with some mugs; as she did, she said, 'So you're Cyril's messenger boy. What's that like?'

Frank smiled. 'I wouldn't know.'

Miss Austin narrowed her eyes and looked at him carefully. 'Don't I recognise you?'

'I shouldn't think so.'

'I'm sure I've seen your face somewhere.'

Frank shrugged. 'I should say,' he said, 'that my message isn't for you, but it involves you, if you know what I mean.'

'I don't think I do.'

'It's for Cyril's wife. Mrs Austin.'

'Sandie?'

'Yes.'

'So why come round here?' Miss Austin's eyes glanced at the ceiling, and she licked her lips.

'Because she's here,' Frank said.

'What?' Her voice was up now, her face muscles rippled and her fingers tightened.

'I know she is.'

'Who the hell are you?'

'Frank.'

'Yeah, but Frank who?'

'I know,' said a voice from behind the door, and Sandie walked into the kitchen. She was wearing jeans and a loose white shirt knotted at the waist. She had untidy hair and was carrying a basket of dirty washing. She put it on the floor and said, 'I've been waiting to meet you.'

Frank stood up. He felt awkward now. He was used to cases ending tidily.

'What's going on?' said Miss Austin.

'Are you going to tell her, or shall I?' said Sandie.

'I think I should; you'll appreciate the new ending.'

'Will I?'

'I think so.'

'Okay.'

Frank sat down again and crossed his legs. Sandie sat opposite and Miss Austin made the tea. As it brewed, he said, 'Two weeks ago, your husband asked us to tail you; he was suspicious. New perfume, new clothes, something about your face he hadn't noticed before; he gave us all the details. He was bothered. I think he'd done a bit of snooping himself, but he couldn't work it out. You'd drop the kids off, you'd shop, you'd come round here, stay a few hours, maybe go to the cinema, then back to pick the kids up. But he was convinced.' Frank rubbed his knees. 'I think deceiving people sweat their deceit, and I think he thinks so too. I sussed you a couple of days ago, and was going to give your husband the real report today.' Frank reached into his pocket. 'And the bill.'

'The real report?' said Sandie. She was thinking about her kids and she was thinking about her husband's temper. She could see walls falling down, and plates flying through the air. Miss Austin moved to her, and laid a hand on her shoulder.

'Yes,' said Frank, 'but this morning I got new orders.'

'From him?'

'No. These were from Bob.'

'Bob?'

'My boss. He told me to give you this' — he gave Sandie the book — 'then I'm to tell your husband that the two of you have been studying this — Tai Chi — together, and give him this.' He held up Bob's report. 'It explains everything. You'd better read it; you don't want to be caught out.'

'You're joking!'

'I am not.'

'Tai Chi?' said Miss Austin.

'Yes.'

'And that's it?'

'For me, yes.'

The two women had known each other for years, but had only discovered their love during the summer. Neither had known passion like it. They felt like two rivers in flood meeting in a parched gorge.

Miss Austin ruffled Sandie's hair and began to pour the tea. 'So your boss; this was his idea?' she said.

'Yes,' said Frank.

'Why? Cyril hired you…'

'I don't know. We're not supposed to make judgement calls, but Bob, he came in and he'd made his mind up. Mr Austin was wrong, you two were right, Mr Austin gets the bill and a lie. One more lie in a world of lies, and no one gets hurt. Bob's always been a bit of a philosopher, but he's getting it bad now.'

'It sounds good to me,' said Sandie.

'I thought it would,' said Frank, and he cupped his tea in his hands, 'but that didn't stop me wondering.'

Bob began with A—G. He emptied the filing cabinet, tipping the contents into a pile he made in the middle of the office floor. Old cases spilled over ones they'd had last year; here was Mr Baxter's request for a bug-sweep of his offices, there was a letter from a Foxwell's Curtains and Blinds about a set of missing keys. Bob picked it up, read it and shook his head. So much paper and so many examples of greed and idiocy. He was not an old man, but he would be if he stayed another week. He reached for drawer H—P, pulled it out and dropped it on his foot. He yelled in pain, kicked out at the pile of paper, and fell over. Memos and invoices covered his legs; he swept some away but others took their place. The phone rang. 'No,' he hissed, and he reached out, grabbed its wire and wrenched it from the wall. 'Go away,' he said, and he put his head in his hands and wept.

Frank looked at his mobile. He shook it, pressed recall and got unobtainable. He dialled his home and the number rang. He hung up, took a last look at Miss Austin's house and drove away.

He reached Mr Austin's office twenty minutes later. He tried the agency again, but it was still dead.

Mr Austin's secretary was talking to a colleague about hygiene when Frank walked in; she adjusted her glasses as he introduced himself. She buzzed his particulars and invited him to take a seat; he had just settled into a copy of *Country Life* when Austin came from an inner office and beckoned him. The secretary watched the two men; when they had gone, she turned to her colleague and said, 'It's a yeast problem.'

Austin was thickening. Once he had been a slim man, a keen squash player and moderate drinker; now he was changing, and the changes bred paranoia and a thick neck. He settled himself behind his desk and asked Frank to sit down.

'Thank you,' said Frank.

'You've got a result?'

'Yes.' Frank put the report on the desk. 'It's all in there.'

'Tell me.'

'Mr Austin —' said Frank, and he cleared his throat with a dramatic hack, 'what I'm going to tell you will probably come as a surprise to you — it came as a surprise to me — but we've been very thorough in our investigations, so believe me.'

'Tell me,' said Austin.

'Your wife is studying Tai Chi with your sister,' said Frank, and as the words came out, he felt the weight of their lie and the pain they balanced upon.

'What?' said Austin.

'Your wife is studying Tai Chi with—'

'Yes. I heard you the first time.'

'And that's the story.' He reached into his pocket and took out the bill. He put it on the desk. 'Our invoice,' he said.

'Tai Chi?'

'Yes.'

'The Chinese exercise?'

'That's the one.'

Austin swivelled in his chair, tipped his head back, pursed his fingers, made a point out of his fingers, and rested his chin on them. He sat like this for a minute, then turned, looked Frank straight in the eyes and said, 'With my sister?'

'Yes.' Frank was tired of this. He was tired of the deceit and irritated by Mr Austin. The man thought he was important, with his tie-pin, his leather chairs and his locked decanters. He wanted power over people, and Frank had been colluding with him. Now it satisfied Frank to think that he was worried and confused.

'You've times and places?'

'All there.' He tapped the report.

'I see,' said Austin.

Frank stood up, took a step towards the door and said, 'If you need us again, you know the number.'

Austin nodded, but didn't say anything. He had turned back to resting his chin on his fingers, and was staring at the ceiling.

An hour later, Frank got back to the office. He found Bob lying on a pile of paper, mumbling about how fish don't lie. 'Fish don't lie, they can't lie, can they? Why should they want to? Oh yes, I know all about you fish.'

Frank bent down, picked up an empty whisky bottle, put it on the littered desk and put an arm on his friend's shoulder. Bob stiffened at the touch, stopped talking, then relaxed. He felt his head vomit, and then it was clear. He sat up.

'What happened?' said Frank.

'I was clearing out.'

'Clearing out what?'

Bob put his hand out and picked up a piece of paper. He read it, screwed it up and threw it down. 'This...'

'Why?'

'... my life.'

Sudden change, unexpected raging, upset Frank, and the worst change was the strange happening to friends. He felt unequipped; all he could think about was the look of amazement on the Austin women's faces, and the look of suspicion and disbelief on Mr Austin's face, and the holes in the deceit, and Bob started crying, and then he was dribbling and talking about fish again. Frank liked the simple life, the uncomplicated day and quiet nights following quiet nights. He liked a small drink, but didn't like to see whole bottles going down at once. And he didn't like to see confusion; you never knew where it was coming from, and what it was going to do. He bent down, took Bob by the arm and lifted him up. Bob had this idea that some trout was out to get him; 'I know what you're looking at, you fish,' he burbled.

Frank said, 'I'm taking you home.'

'Home,' said Bob.

'Yes.'

'Fish live in the sea.'

'And in lakes,' said Frank, as he steered his friend around the piles of paper, kicking at a wastepaper-basket and grabbing his hat and coat as he passed through the outer office.

'Oh yes. Lakes and rivers,' said Bob. 'Lakes and rivers.'

4

Frank put Bob to bed, made a cup of coffee and sat down to watch afternoon television. He saw the last twenty minutes of an old episode of *Dallas*, then went for a game-show. Contestants from Finland, Denmark, Belgium, France, UK, Ireland, Spain and Portugal answered questions about food, farm animals and history; Frank snapped it off after ten minutes and looked for something to read. There was a pile of old fishing magazines on the sofa, some travel brochures and a copy of *Exchange & Mart*. He picked this up and flicked through it. Cheap office equipment, second-hand air compressors, unusual pets and a hundred different ways of making a lot of money. Personalised pens and key-rings, land in Spain and holidays in Jersey. Frank turned to the motoring section and thought, for a minute, about buying a new car. The thought passed when he heard Bob moaning, and the sound of retching and bed springs.

He heard his friend get up and go to the bathroom; taps were run and a cupboard door opened and closed.

The sound of bath taps running was a comfort to Frank. When he had been a child, frightening nights were sometimes relieved by light under the bathroom door and the sound of his mother running taps. The sound made him feel warm and remembered, and cared for. He sat down again, picked up a newspaper and read half an article about plastic surgery. He studied some before-and-after photographs, and thought about his nose. He'd known a few noses in his life; noses like chisels and noses like tomatoes, noses that ran and noses in the air. He heard Bob sigh and then start to hum.

The vet arrived as Mrs Platt was putting the kettle on for a cup of tea; he took one look at the bird and knew that it had only a few days to live. Its feathers were hanging off it like weeds, and its one sad, open eye had turned milky. Mrs Platt tapped the top of the cage and said, 'He's such a good friend.'

'They can be,' said the vet. He was a young man. He enjoyed the variety of his work, and the fact that he was always welcome in other people's homes. He loved relieving worry and pain, and the trust the work bred. His favourite animals were cats, and the most difficult to treat were invertebrates. Once, he had an oyster as a patient, an enormous thing that lived in a salt-water tank with a lobster. The oyster's owner claimed that it was depressed, a diagnosis rooted in madness. The vet had tasted the water and said that it was too salty; what a stroke of genius! The owner had changed the water immediately, and the oyster had cheered up.

The vet was happy in his work, and he was also in love with a dental nurse called Cheryl. Every time he thought about her, his brain throbbed and the blood in his legs slowed and buzzed in its veins. She filled his head and all the things he did. Every time he saw her, he felt the hairs on his head sing and the palms of his hands walk. When he kissed her, he felt as though his whole world could slip away and disappear in her, and he felt the warm hands of chaos playing with his heart.

'Is he very ill?' said Mrs Platt.

'I'm afraid so,' said the vet. He opened the cage and put his hand inside. Joey attempted to back off, but all his hopes and all his primeval dreams were betraying him. The flock of budgies he had been roosting with had flown south, heading towards the coast. They would rest in a corn field before flying on.

'Is there anything you can do for him?'

'I don't know.' The vet had Joey in his hand now; he took him from the cage and turned him over. 'Maybe,' he said, 'but I'd guess he's quite an old bird…' he stroked it under the chin, 'aren't you?'

'I've had him about ten years.'

'That long?'

Mrs Platt nodded.

'I have to tell you that he's one of the oldest budgerigars I've come across; he's lucky to have lived this long.'

'Oh dear.'

'I'm sorry.'

Mrs Platt had to turn away from the vet. He was a nice young man with a kind voice and clean fingernails. She picked up a piece of cuttlefish and picked at its edges; as she did, the vet held Joey's head between the forefinger and index finger of his right hand, and snapped the bird's neck. Then he put the body in the cage, propped it against a water bowl and closed the door. 'I have to say,' he said, and he picked up his case, 'that I don't think he's got more than a few hours left.'

'Is he in pain?'

'No.'

'Are you sure?'

'As long as you keep him quiet and warm.'

Mrs Platt turned back to look at Joey. The bird looked happier than it had done before she'd called the vet; it was resting its head against the bars of the cage. She was pleased that she'd done the right thing. You must look after your pets. You must not let them suffer.

Bob came from the bathroom wearing a dressing-gown. He went to the kitchen, filled a kettle and said, 'Coffee?'

'Thanks,' said Frank, and, 'How are you feeling?'

Bob stood in the kitchen door. 'Better. Did you bring me home?'

'Yes; but I let you trash the office first.'

'Did I?'

'You did.'

'Mmm.'

'Why, Bob?' Frank put on his biggest stare, and pursed his lips. 'What's going on?'

Bob absent-mindedly scratched his crotch and shook his head. 'What can I say?'

'Cut the bullshit and tell me straight.'

'That's what you want?'

'Yes.'

'I'm not sure.'

'Bob!'

The kettle began to boil, Bob took a step back into the kitchen.

'Forget the coffee!' Frank was angry now. He didn't want lies. Life had to make sense. He had to have it neat, with hospital corners and folded pyjamas. He wanted reasons, he wanted to know where he stood, and he wanted his friends to trust him. Deceit bred chaos, and chaos was Frank's greatest fear. He wanted phones to work, Volvic to taste sweet and Mrs Platt's budgie to cheep. He needed Lisa to tell him her news, and he needed the *News at Ten*. 'Tell me!' he shouted. 'Bottles of whisky in the afternoon, lying to Austin, wrecking the office; you want me to do the work, but it's hard—'

'Hard?' Bob laughed. 'You think it's hard?'

'Yes.'

'Then do what I'm doing.'

'And what's that?'

'I'm jacking it in…' said Bob, and he turned around, went to the kettle and switched it off.

Frank didn't say anything for a minute. 'I'm jacking it in…' floated in the air, riding a thermal that rose from Bob's head, always out of reach, but always visible. The words were solid, they were meant and they were clear. Frank examined them, trying to see them from all angles, but he couldn't. They were in his head, they were in the air, they twisted around, he could not understand them. They confused him and made him nervous. He heard Bob fiddle with some mugs, but the noise didn't disturb his thoughts. They trundled on, travelling down a straight track, unable to deviate. They struggled with confusion and they fought his nerves; Bob came back with the coffees, put them on the floor and said, 'I've had enough.'

Frank didn't like mugs of coffee on the floor; he picked his up and held it in front of him.

'Did you hear me, Frank?'

His name came out of a trance; he looked up and said, 'You've had enough?'

'Yes.'

'Why?'

Now Bob laughed and said, 'Austin. He made me realise. You think we've had to lie to him, but we've been lying to his wife and sister for a fortnight.'

'How's that?'

'Think about it.'

'I have, but I know I'm off your track.'

'All our sitting outside the house, following them into cinemas, watching them walk along the beach; that's lying. Deceit. What business is it of ours? If Austin can't sort his own problems, if he can't take a day off from the office and treat his wife like a human being, if he can't see trouble coming, then what the hell does he expect? What do he and all the other fuckers we've worked for expect? And what do we expect? Ten per cent discount for early settlement?'

'We're providing a service,' said Frank, steadily.

Bob laughed again.

'People need us.'

'People need us when they can't be bothered themselves.'

'That's bullshit. We've got expertise. Skills.'

'Expertise my arse. Anyone could do our jobs. Think about it; if you can sit in a car you can be a Private. Maybe it helps if you can write, but it's not important. A mobile and a second-hand car, and you're away.'

'You…' said Frank, but he couldn't catch any more words. They were stacked in his mind but wouldn't go to his mouth. He drank some coffee, glanced at his old friend and looked out of the window. A streetlamp tinted the sky orange, and a fluorescing seagull flew by. Flurries of snow blew against the windows, catching in the corners and climbing up the glass. Bob's place was above a newsagent; the top of a Christmas tree was level with the sill. Frank could see a pink fairy's back, a yellow light flashing on the top of her wand.

'I'm selling,' said Bob, 'and I'm going to relax. Read a few books, watch some telly, sit in the bath a lot. Maybe I'll go on holiday. I think Tunisia's nice at this time of year. It's cheap too.' He smiled at the thought; the sun, the camels, the sand in his hair and the busy bazaars. 'Everyone owes themselves some time.'

'You've got it worked out?' Frank had wanted to sound sarcastic, but Bob heard statement of fact delivered in a level tone of voice.

'I certainly have,' said Bob.

'When? When's this happening?'

'As soon as I find a buyer. Maybe you'd be interested.'

'Me?'

'Why not?'

'No,' said Frank, and he'd had enough. He stood up and picked up his coat. 'No,' he said again, and he went to the door.

'Frank?' said Bob.

Frank stopped and looked around.

'You okay?'

'Okay?'

'Yes.'

Frank shook his head in despair, and let himself out. He stood on the street for five minutes and let snow cover his head. Some children were skidding down the pavement on plastic sacks, shouting and throwing snowballs. Frank watched them and thought, We are not children, we are adults. Our lives are not games, we were not born to play. Then he thought about Lisa, and how she would be coming in from a day at the chemist's, smelling of TCP and lozenges. She'd be looking forward to meeting Adrian in a pub, and enjoying a drink in comfort. She would glow with happiness, smiling at the perfect way her life was developing. She would come home later and smile at him over a late cup of tea; oh yes, thought Frank, how simple life might be.

5

At half-past six Frank let himself into Mrs Platt's house, stamped his feet on the mat, checked the hall table for post and began to climb the stairs. He had his left foot on the third step when Mrs Platt put her head around the door and said, 'Usual time tonight, Frank?' He listened for her bird, but heard nothing. 'Joey's not been well,' she said, 'but the vet came and he's been better since. He's asleep at the moment.'

'Asleep?' said Frank.

'Yes. Do you want to see him? He looks so peaceful.'

Frank was feeling very tired, but he couldn't say no to Mrs Platt. Her smile grabbed him and would not let go. It shook him until he rattled. He climbed back down the stairs and followed her into her rooms.

Her rooms were dark and smelt of cabbage, mothballs and candle wax. There were antimacassars on chairs, pictures of uniformed men on the walls and lace curtains at the windows. Frank was suddenly, inexplicably, attacked by the memory of a woman he thought he had loved, but he'd been mistaken. He'd left his heart for lust, he'd allowed himself to become trapped by the random flight of desire. As Mrs Platt led him to Joey's cage, he remembered. The woman's mother had lived in rooms like these, rooms from a time when skin was sin, Christ was king, tradesmen called at side doors and little men mended your car when it broke down. Pianos with brass candle-holders stood in rooms that were never used, and Paris was days away. Sherry was dusty and beer died in the glass; a dead and terrible time, a false construction that bled itself to death.

'Look,' said Mrs Platt.

A lie, Christian fakery. Order, thought Frank, came from people, and chaos was God's work.

'Frank?'

'I'm sorry,' he said, and he went to stand next to Mrs Platt. They stared at Joey together, and the first thing he thought was — the bird is dead.

'Doesn't he look happy?' said Mrs Platt.

Frank wondered. Agree and keep her happy, tell the truth and dismay her. His mouth decided. 'Yes,' he said.

'The vet was such a nice man,' she said, smiling. She had false teeth; the top plate dropped down. She clicked it back into place. 'You know what he did?'

'No.'

'He had Joey out of his cage, and he was treating him like one of his own. He's got healing hands.'

Frank looked carefully at Joey, and he knew the bird was dead. Dead things give off no air, no colour and a flat, high smell. They are finished.

'He's very tired,' said Mrs Platt, 'aren't you?' She tapped the cage with her fingernails. The bird slipped so its beak was resting against the water bowl.

'I think we ought to let him sleep,' said Frank.

Mrs Platt put her hand on his arm and said, 'You're right.' She led him to the door. As he was about to leave her rooms and go upstairs, she said, 'You're such a nice man, Frank.'

'Thank you,' he said. Once, the compliment would have pleased him, but now he barely noticed it. But he remembered how he would have been pleased, and he recognised his indifference, and the memory of the woman attacked him again. Janet Black, Minehead, 1959, Rock 'n' Roll, boots of Spanish leather, Butlins, snooker and Ray Butts. Ray Butts, Janet Black and Butlins. Minehead. Elvis. The boots that did not work. Frank climbed the steps to his flat and did not stop outside Lisa's. He did not stop until he was sitting in a chair by the window with a bottle of Volvic in his hands. Then, as the night froze and the stars were covered with clouds, he closed his eyes.

Lisa and Adrian were sitting in a pub. They had chosen a quiet corner. She was drinking a dry Martini and tonic, he had a pint. She had lemon but no ice, he had the threat of a paunch. She was a spark, he was stupid. She was full of joy, he was scared. He stared at his drink and thought about Carlisle. He had a friend there she knew nothing about, a mechanic. This friend had told him that Carlisle was all right, and that there was plenty of work. Adrian decided to lie to Lisa and tell his friend the truth. He would play along with her, and then disappear. She looked at him with her loving eyes and wanted to hold him so close. She wanted to know when they were getting married, and she wanted to know if she could move in with him straight away. She said she wanted to get used to being with him all the time, she wanted to go shopping for groceries with him. He felt too warm, and wanted to go outside for a breath of fresh air.

She followed him, and they stood on the pavement together. Their breath plumed in the cold night, and her eyes watered. She put her arm around him and tucked herself into his side; he put his arm across her shoulders, but he did not mean it. He did not squeeze her, or look at her. Yesterday she had been a lay but now she was not. For a second, he thought that he would tell her there, outside in the pub in the freezing cold. Then the second went. Say nothing and go.

Janet Black, Minehead, Ray Butts, boots of Spanish leather; these memories drained from Frank's head when he heard Lisa come home; he picked up Miriam Stoppard's book and read for twenty minutes and then started to make a pot of tea. Five minutes later he hid the book under the sink as she climbed the stairs to his place. Before she could knock, he called out, 'Come in, Lisa, it's open.'

She sat down and he poured her a cup of tea. She was subdued; he said, 'You okay?'

She nodded, sipped her tea, said, 'That's better,' and 'Adrian dropped me off.' He drove an old car. 'He was quiet tonight.'

Frank crossed his legs and looked serious. 'Pregnancy,' he said, 'can be as traumatic for the father as it is for the mother. Many men feel jealous, they feel their woman has been taken over by something they can't control, and—'

'Frank,' said Lisa, 'you sound like a guidebook!'

'Do I?'

'Yeah, you do.' She laughed at him, and he felt his face tingle.

'Sorry.'

'Don't be.' She sipped some more tea. 'It's good to know someone's interested.'

'Adrian's interested.'

'How do you know?'

'Isn't he?'

'I wonder.'

'I thought he was over the moon.'

'So did I.'

'What you're feeling,' said Frank, and his serious face came again, 'is not unusual. Mothers-to-be often experience feelings of insecurity. You might even begin to feel—'

'You have been reading something!'

'No I haven't,' he blurted. 'Nothing.' The lie was out before the truth had a chance to get its shoes on; it was left standing in his brain with its mouth open.

' A whole lot of nothing, Frank?'

'I know a lot about a lot of things,' he said. 'It's my job.'

'You staked out a maternity unit today?'

'No, but I wish I had.' Frank's voice betrayed his confusion; he tried to control it but failed.

'Why?'

'You don't want to know.'

'Tell me.'

Frank could not refuse Lisa. When he looked at her, he imagined her as a baby in the wrong man's arms. She could have been his. They deserved each other. He sighed, took a deep breath and then began to tell her about Austin, Bob, Tai Chi, piles of paper and more stuff about Bob. He made some more tea, and listened as she told him that you can never be sure about people, however well you think you know them. One minute they're there and the next they're gone. Or one minute they tell you something you can't believe, but that thing has been the truth for as long as you've known them. She said that she thought the secret of life was control, and he liked that. Then she looked at her watch and said that she had to go to bed. He agreed and apologised for keeping her up with her troubles, and told her that she was sleeping for two now. He offered to walk her to her door, but she said that it was only ten stairs.

6

Frank was up early. The sun was showing for the first time in a week; its pale light reflected off the snowy roofs and began to melt the lines of icicles that ran beneath the gutters. He showered, shaved and ate breakfast listening to the radio news. On his way down, he stopped for a moment outside Lisa's door. He heard nothing, so he carried on and was letting himself out when Mrs Platt put her head around her door and said, 'Joey's still asleep.'

'Joey?'

'Yes,'

'Of course,' said Frank.

'Do you think I should try and wake him up?'

Frank thought about this. 'No,' he said. 'Let him rest. He was probably awake during the night; he'll get up in his own good time.'

Mrs Platt nodded. Frank was right. He left the house, stood on the step, buttoned his coat, took a deep breath of morning air and drove to work.

Bob slept late. When he arrived at the office, Frank was waiting for him. He had tidied the files away, thrown two empty whisky bottles in the bin, and opened the windows. He'd gone over the floor with a vacuum cleaner, wiped down the desks and made a cup of tea. He was looking through Cases Pending when Bob arrived. 'Hell,' he said, 'it's freezing in here.'

Frank got up and closed the windows. 'The place stank.'

'That's what places do,' said Bob, and he sat down with his coat on, and held his collar.

'You look like shit.'

'I feel like shit. I am shit.'

'No,' said Frank, 'you're confused.'

'Thank you, doctor.'

'What do you want me to say?'

'Confused. You said that.'

'And you're feeling sorry for yourself.'

'Who else is going to?'

'You need someone to?'

'Who doesn't, Frank? Don't you? When you sit up there in your room, sipping water and talking to your girlfriend…'

'She's not my girlfriend,' Frank snapped.

'… and talking to your girlfriend, don't you ever wish that she'd take your head, put it on her little shoulder and stroke your worries away, tell you that she understands why you're tired?'

'Lisa and I…'

'Because you do get tired, don't you, Frank?' Bob's face hovered between smiling and grief, not sure which way to jump. 'Say you do.'

Frank looked at his friend and closed his eyes. He remembered what life had been like three days before. He'd left the office secure in the knowledge that life was secure. It was winter, Mrs Platt was a fair landlady, Bob could have no complaints, he'd seen a teapot in the shape of an old-fashioned kitchen range that would make a perfect Christmas present for Lisa. Volvic was drawn from springs that rose in the heart of France. He opened his eyes, and now he wondered if Volvic was a lie. Maybe it came from Ireland, and its sweet taste came from peat it filtered through, not volcanic rock. Confusion was contagious. It was a disease, the easiest to catch. It was enough to look at it; you can catch it as easily as that. Then you were two stops from confusion's father. Chaos was waiting for you on the platform, with his whips, his pierced ears and his enormous eyes. Frank's vision was out of focus; Bob was a blur of beige, the office was squares of colour. Bob snapped his fingers and said, 'Frank?'

'Bob?' Frank focused. He had not been dreaming.

'One.' Bob held up one finger. 'What I said last night; I meant it. You've got first refusal on this place,' he spread his arms, 'otherwise, I'm putting it on the market. Two.' He held up a second finger. 'I don't want to tell you what to do today. From now on, I'm treading water.'

'Treading water?'

'Yes.'

'Is there a three?'

'No, That's it.'

Frank swivelled in his chair, stood up and walked to the window. He said, 'It still stinks in here,' and opened it. He leant out. People were shopping in the street below, walking carefully between piles of slush. From where he stood, they looked so simple and unconcerned. As they passed, they all seemed to know each other. Some stopped to talk, others nodded, a few walked hand in hand. From a height, nothing seemed wrong; everything, even in chaos, seemed ordered. He watched two babies in their pushchairs. They were dressed in mittens, thick coats and woollen hats. One of them was crying; this set the other off, and their pained cries rose to where Frank was leaning, but when they reached him they sounded like song. Nothing, he thought, is what it seems. He turned around and said to Bob, 'Either do something useful or go home.'

'I'll go home,' said Bob, and he did.

Lisa phoned Adrian from work, but his boss said he'd gone out. The boss was angry; Adrian had said he had to go to the dentist. That was two hours ago, and now they had a rush job on a Volvo.

'Dentist?' said Lisa.

'Yeah,' said the boss, and hung up.

He'd said nothing about the dentist to her. Last time she'd seen his teeth, they'd looked white and even. His breath had smelt of mint, and he hadn't held his jaw and moaned. 'The dentist?' she said to the buzzing receiver, then she put it down. She stared at it. It accused Adrian, but she didn't notice. His face, his words and his promises filled her head. She put her hand on her belly. She listened. Her embryonic fluid was singing. Her heart filled and all her dreams flowed into her desires as a woman came into the shop and asked for some aspirin and a comb. Lisa was helpful and the woman left the shop with exactly what she wanted. Lisa was meeting Adrian at seven; she would remember to take him some aspirins, in case his teeth were hurting.

At half-past eleven, Mrs Platt decided to wake Joey and offer him some seed. She tapped the bars of his cage, and when he didn't move, she opened his door. She put her hand in and tickled him under the chin. His head dropped, he slumped forward, held this new position for a second and then fell over. As he lay on his side, Mrs Platt picked him up and took him from the cage. She held his head in her fingers and puckered her lips at his beak; 'Joey love,' she said, 'it's Mummy.'

Joey did not move.

'Do you want something to eat?'

Joey was cold.

'You're cold,' she said, and then the truth began to dawn. It came from behind her, carrying lilies, spreading its arms and smiling insincerely. It had blood around its mouth, and its teeth were made from cuttlefish. She looked at Joey's eyes, and they would not open; she noticed a circle of mucus around his nose, and the unnatural clench of his claws, and she remembered what the vet had said. 'He hasn't got more than a few hours left.' Mrs Platt knew Joey was dead, and this hit her. She staggered backwards and stumbled towards an armchair; she tripped on its legs, put her left hand out to break her fall and dropped the bird. He bounced once then lay on a small Persian rug, his wings tucked in tight to his body and his head bent back. Mrs Platt grabbed a standard lamp and pulled it down on top of her. It crashed down, the bulb exploded and the room went dark. She lay on her back with the lamp across her stomach, one of her legs pushed back under the chair and the other stretched out. She felt faint, she felt watery, and her mind flashed a hundred images of her life in straight sequence. Her mother, her father, her brothers, her sisters and all the things they did. The house she lived in now when it was a family house with servants and bells in every room connected to the pantry and steaming ranges and tradesmen in caps calling with baskets of fresh produce. School, courting, Mr Platt, the war, her first Joey and the five Joeys since. A piece of hot glass had fallen on her last Joey and had singed his feathers. The smell of burning tinted the air. Mrs Platt's right leg hurt. She closed her eyes, and that made everything better. She felt as though she were swimming, something she had never enjoyed before, but now it was pleasant. Warm water, darkness and sympathy.

Frank spent the day with the telephone and Cases Pending, and tried to organise Bob's organisation. Bob had a system based on colours; urgent work was coded with a red dot, less urgent with a yellow, even less urgent with a blue, then a green, and a purple. Personal documents were dotted white, and office invoices/receipts, black. This was a system that worked; its practicalities demanded understanding and tolerance, and in the morning, in the hour after Bob had left to go home, Frank determined to master it, but by noon he was confused.

Working through the red dots, he discovered one file dated 24 February 1987, and another that contained nothing but garage receipts for the year 1990–91. Then he found Mr Austin's correspondence in a blue file, and a back copy of *Go Fishing!* in a black, Bob, whose system had developed over many years, knew why *Go Fishing!* was in a black, but he was not the sort of man who explained the obvious. He had been waiting all his life to act on an impulse, and he was not going to clutter his reasons with anything. Explanations, excuses, regret, cold sweats and cigarette burns; life was too short. He had discovered an appetite, and few people really do that.

Between a red file stuffed with pages torn from *Exchange & Mart,* and a purple file full of used stamps, the phone rang. For a moment, Frank waited for Bob to enter the office and answer it, but after three rings he remembered, he smoothed his chin, he took a deep breath and answered it.

'Frank?'

'Bob?'

'Yeah,' said Bob. He was sitting in the bath with a bottle of beer and the radio on. 'What are you doing?'

'Working.'

'Why?' said Bob, and he hung up.

7

At half-past five, as the air began to bite after the day's thaw, Frank let himself into Mrs Platt's house, stamped his feet on the mat and checked the hall table for post. There was a hand-delivered letter waiting for Lisa. He began to climb the stairs, but when he had passed the fifth he stopped.

He stood and waited. He listened to his watch ticking, and he heard a pipe gurgle above him. The sound drifted down and he thought he heard words in it. Nothing specific, and nothing Mrs Platt would say. He retraced his steps and rang her bell. When there was no reply, he put his ear to the door and said, 'Mrs Platt?'

There was silence.

'Mrs Platt? Hello?'

Nothing.

He waited for a moment, then tried the door. It was unlocked. He let it swing open, stood on the threshold and said, 'Mrs Platt?' again. Her name floated into the room, bounced around the furniture and settled on a mantelpiece. He turned on the light and saw her lying on the floor.

He ran to her, and knelt down. He put his ear to her nose and listened. She was breathing, the air fluttering out of her body like wings. 'Mrs Platt,' he said, and he straightened her arm. He put his hand under her head and she moved her right leg. She winced, opened her eyes and said, 'Joey?'

'No,' said Frank. 'It's Frank.'

'Frank?'

'From upstairs.'

'Oh,' she wheezed, 'Frank.'

'What happened, Mrs Platt?'

She lifted her hand and pointed across the floor. 'Joey's dead. I couldn't help him.'

Frank looked at the dead bird, nodded slowly and whispered, 'I'm sorry.'

Mrs Platt tried to sit up, but slipped back.

'Steady,' said Frank. He righted the standard lamp and stood it to one side, put an arm around her shoulders and the other around her waist. He could feel her bones shivering through her skin. 'I'm going to lift you up. Okay?'

'Thank you.'

He sat her in an armchair.

'Comfortable?'

She rubbed her arms. 'Nothing broken.' She looked at the lamp. 'Apart from that, I think.'

'It's just the bulb.'

'And Joey,' she said.

'I'm sure,' said Frank, and he felt stupidity rise in him, 'he didn't feel any pain. He's gone to a better place.'

'Do you think so?' said Mrs Platt.

'Yes.'

She put her hand on his shoulder and squeezed. She was crying.

'Come upstairs and I'll make you a cup of tea. Plenty of sugar.'

'Oh, Frank,' she said, 'you're kind.'

Frank gave Mrs Platt a cup of tea and as she drank she began to talk about Whitby and the Yorkshire coast. She made him promise to take her there one day. She said she would treat him to a weekend at the guest-house she used to stay in. She could picture it, standing on a cliff with a view of the church, the sea and the harbour. She told him that the town was full of fish restaurants. This made him sit up. 'Just you and me,' she said, 'and when we get back I can buy another Joey.' Frank was pleased that she was able to talk about buying another bird, and she wiped her eyes, told him that the tea was the best she'd drunk for a week, and could she have a cake? She had seen a box of French Fancies on the side. 'Of course you can,' said Frank, and he fetched them.

Three hours later, as Mrs Platt slept in her rooms and Frank brushed his teeth, he heard the street door slam shut. Lisa had arranged to meet Adrian in the pub, but he hadn't turned up. She'd waited two hours, tapping her watch, drinking Martinis and watching couples. Couples are happy to a single person, even if they're arguing. They're together, and that's what counts. Some were arguing, others were staring into each other's eyes, blamelessly counting stars. Lisa felt blameless and angry.

As she stood in the hall and stamped the slush off her shoes, she saw the letter. She picked it up and held it to her nose. It smelt of Swarfega. It was Adrian's smell and his writing. He had never written to her before, and now, as she held the envelope in her hand, an idea careered out of nowhere. She felt her organs wilt and her skin creep. She knew as soon as she saw her name in his crooked writing, and she knew why she had sat alone for two hours. Her eyes told her, and her stomach, and the anger she had burned in the pub exploded into fury. She ran up the stairs, ripping the envelope open as she went. She unlocked her door, kicked it open and threw her coat on the floor. 'Okay,' she said, 'tell me.'

Dear Lisa, This is the hardest letter I have written because I do think about you and think your great, but I cannot get married any more because I have got another job, and its not in Brighton. I know you will think I am a real bastard for this but I had to tell you now because I cannot go through with it. I know you are going to have a baby and I wanted to see it when it's born but I have promised this friend that I will be working for him, and I can't let him down. I hope you understand, but I had to say this now, I didn't want to say it later, when it's too late. I will let you know where I am, and then I'll phone. Is it alright? Love, Adrian.

Lisa screamed 'All right!' She screwed the letter into a ball, then grabbed an empty coffee mug and threw it at the wall. She kicked a table leg, yelled 'All right?' again, and saw a teapot she had given him. It was in the shape of a football. It was next to go, exploding in a shower of china over the sofa. 'Bastard!' She went to the kitchen, grabbed a bottle of whisky from a shelf, unscrewed it and threw the cap across the room.

Frank was out of his flat the moment the mug was thrown, and was standing at her open door as she took her first swig.

'Lisa?' He knocked once, then walked in. He found her standing by the kitchen sink, one hand on the bottle and the other to her eyes. 'Lisa?'

'What?'

'Are you all right?'

Se turned to face him. 'What the fuck does it look like?'

'What happened?'

'Adrian.'

'What about him?'

She turned around again and hissed, 'It's in there!'

'What's in there?'

'His letter.'

Frank went back into the sitting-room, picked up the letter, unscrewed it and read it. Lisa came out and slumped on the sofa; he sat down next to her, took the bottle from her hand and whispered, 'Lisa.'

'Oh yeah,' she said, 'Lisa...'

'I'm sorry.'

'Of course you are, Frank. You're always sorry, aren't you?'

Frank took it. 'I know, and I mean it every time.'

'People who say they're sorry all the time...' and she snatched the bottle back and took another swig, 'never have anything to be really sorry about. Usually, they're the ones who haven't done anything. Non-achievers. They're apologising for themselves, not for something they've done.' She wiped her mouth with the back of her hand, smearing a line of lipstick across her cheek. 'Is that you, Frank?'

He took the bottle back, stared at the label, tried to peel its top corner and opened his mouth.

'I bet you're the type who says sorry when someone steps on your foot.'

'Lisa...'

'Don't.' She snatched the bottle back.

'I think you're—'

'Don't!'

'I wasn't going to do anything.'

'There!' she cried. 'Either you do nothing or you say you're sorry.' She swigged. 'You're useless. You, him, my old man, the boss. Men.' She snorted. 'Worthless.'

'Do you want me to go?'

'Do what you want.'

'I'll stay.'

'Steady!' She glared at him. Her eyes were filmy and the pupils dilated. 'You don't want to be decisive.'

'I'll stay,' he repeated, 'if you share the bottle.'

'That's right. Nothing's for nothing, eh, Frank?'

'I didn't say that.'

'But you meant to.'

'I didn't.'

'You're a man, aren't you?'

'Yes.'

'You meant it.'

'Not all men are like him.'

'No?'

'No.'

'Prove it.'

Frank thought.

'Prove it.'

Frank took the bottle and swigged. 'I think he must be mad.'

'Why, Frank?'

'Because you're…'

'Yes.'

'I don't know if I…'

'Yes!'

'It's hard for me.'

'Tell me!'

'I think,' said Frank, and he had another drink, 'that you're lovely.' He hadn't said anything like it to a woman for over twenty years, and he heard his voice come as if he was listening from the other side of the room. He cringed.

She laughed. 'Lovely?'

'Yes.'

'Two questions, Frank,' she said. 'What does that prove and do you really think you're getting in my pants?'

Now Frank was angry. He stood up. He'd been where she

was. In 1959, Janet Black had written him a letter like Adrian's. He knew about the deceit that rides on love's back, and had not forgotten. He remembered how a pair of boots, bought to impress Janet, had pinched like hell, and he remembered Ray Butts on his motor bike. 'It proves,' said Frank, slowly and carefully, 'that you're not the sort of woman I'd want.' He licked his lips. 'I heard someone smashing up your place, I didn't know whether it was you, someone else, or someone else attacking you, or what it was; so I came down and all the thanks I get is—'

'You want thanks?'

'I didn't say—'

'Yes you did! You want whisky, you want thanks and what else?'

'I could find him for you.'

'Find him?'

'No trouble.'

Lisa laughed. 'Why? I don't need him.' She put her hand on her stomach. 'We don't need him.'

'No?'

'Or you.'

Frank turned around and slammed the door as he left. He stormed up the stairs, stopped outside his door, then stormed down again, past Lisa's, past Mrs Platt's and into the night.

Frank walked. It was snowing. The streets were empty. Every step he took echoed. He could hear a rushing noise in his ears, like steam escaping. He walked faster. He was not wearing a coat, but he didn't feel cold. Lisa's whisky was burning behind his eyes and twisting his thoughts. Janet Black was in there, talking about him with Bob. Then there was Lisa and Mrs Platt. Each had a different idea about him but they didn't argue, they agreed. He tried to ignore them but he couldn't; they were like a waking dream, accusing, deriding and pointing. 'Prove it!' said Lisa, and Bob said the same. 'Prove you love me,' said Janet Black, and Mrs Platt said, 'You promised to take me to

Whitby.' Promises and proofs. Even the snowflakes whispered as they drifted through the Christmas lights that decorated the deserted streets.

'God,' he said to a parked car. His voice startled him. He stopped walking and stared at the sky, and let the snow murmur over his face. Then he turned east and walked towards the Palace Pier.

Chaos breeds chaos, and Frank could prove that. Twenty-four hours and he had the evidence. He could deliver a report, a bill and go home satisfied, but he was not. He was lost to satisfaction and caught by confusion. He stepped on to the beach beneath the pier, and walked down to the sea.

The water was calm. The waves broke softly, dragged the shingle and rustled it like paper. He picked up a pebble and threw it as far as he could. It's a story that haunts every life that was ever lived, tolling like a bell that will not stop. It sounds across valleys and sounds into the mountains. It crosses oceans and fords rivers. It rides its deceit like a horse, dropping spores of chaos every minute. It's black and it's white, and it's every colour you ever saw. It's weather and it's speech, and its words are unspelt.

8

In the morning, Frank poured a bowl of cereal and listened to the radio news while he ate. The world ran on deceit, and it topped itself up every day. A politician was making excuses for a policy that had never been what it turned out to be. The man's voice soared between one idea of the truth and the truth itself, but didn't touch either. He threatened to tie himself in knots but never did; Frank heard but did not listen. The radio was company, the voice was like a pet in a cage. He switched it off and went out.

He didn't stop outside Lisa's room, but he knocked on Mrs Platt's door. She answered it. She was wearing a quilted dressing-gown.

'Oh, Frank.' She rubbed her eyes, and dabbed at the corners of her mouth with the tips of her fingers. 'I've overslept.'

'Good for you,' he said. 'How are you feeling?'

'I'll be fine.' She touched her hair. 'I'm going to have a wake for Joey. Will you come?'

'This evening?'

'Yes. I'm going to ask Lisa.'

'Okay,' said Frank. 'I'll bring a bottle.'

'And the vet.'

'The vet?'

'He was such a nice man.'

'Oh,' said Frank, and he took a step back.

'Any time after six,' said Mrs Platt.

Two policemen were waiting for Frank. They were sitting in a car outside the office; when he let himself in, they followed him.

'Frank?' said the first.

'Yes.'

'Inspector Evans.' He flipped his card. 'And this is Sergeant Davis. Can we have a word?'

Frank looked at Evans. He started with his feet and worked up. A Christmas carol drifted in the air. 'Why not?' he said.

Frank sat behind Bob's desk. Evans and Davis sat opposite. Evans did the talking, Davis watched carefully. Evans wore a double-breasted suit, a white shirt and a polka-dot tie. Davis wore jeans, a sweat-shirt and training shoes.

'What's happening?' said Frank.

Evans fished for his pocket-book, opened it, flicked some pages, fiddled with a pencil and said, 'Austin. Ring any bells?'

'Austin?'

'You got it.'

'We just finished a job for an Austin.'

'Spence Road?'

'That's him.'

'What was the nature of the job?'

Frank smiled. The policemen held their faces blank. Frank said, 'That's confidential.'

'I don't think so,' said Evans.

Davis didn't move.

'Our clients are guaranteed confidentiality. You know that. It's in our contracts.'

'Is it?' said Evans.

'So unless you can—'

'And your clients are guaranteed a discounted funeral?'

'What are you talking about?'

'You heard.'

'I heard,' said Frank, 'but I didn't understand.'

'Smart, are you?' said Davis.

Evans turned and put his finger to his lips.

'What is this?' said Frank.

'Austin.' Evans coughed. 'You were working for him. We can hold you to that?'

'Sure.'

'And when was the last time you saw him?'

'Yesterday. We'd wrapped up the case, and I went round to—'

'What exactly was the case?'

'He'd asked us to tail his wife. He thought she was cheating on him.'

'And was she?'

Frank turned and looked out of the window.

'Was she?'

'Yes.'

Evans nodded. 'And you told him this?'

'No.'

'No?'

'Yes.'

'What did you tell him?'

'I told him that his wife was studying Tai Chi with his sister.'

'Tai Chi?'

'Yes. It's a Chinese exercise, a sort of meditation…'

'I know. And?'

'That's it.'

Evans nodded, glanced at his colleague and looked back at Frank.

'What's this about?' said Frank.

'Mrs Austin is dead.'

'Murdered. Throat cut.'

'She was found this morning at her house. There'd been no signs of forced entry, no sign of a struggle, nothing stolen; we're extremely anxious to find Mr Austin. We found your card in her handbag, so decided you're as good a place to start as any.' Evans coughed. 'Are you?'

'Dead?'

'Dead.'

'She'd done nothing.'

'That's the way it is.'

'His sister?' said Frank. 'Have you seen her?'

'Austin has a sister?'

'You haven't! Have you even spoken to her?'

'No.'

Frank stood up and grabbed his coat. 'Come on!' he said, and he pulled Evans after him, out of the office and into the street.

Evans drove, Frank sat beside him, Davis sat in the back and stared blankly at Brighton's shops.

'You met Austin?' said Evans.

'A couple of times.'

'What was he like?'

'Efficient. He wanted to have things under control. He didn't like to shake hands, and I remember his eyes. He'd never look directly at you. It was difficult to know what he was thinking.'

'Hiding something?'

'I don't know if it was that. Do you have to be hiding something to be secretive?'

'He was secretive?'

'I don't know.'

'And this sister. You met her at his office?'

Frank laughed, then cut it. 'No.'

'Where?'

'At his wife's. They were sleeping together.'

'His wife was sleeping with his sister?'

'Yes.'

Evans shook his head. 'There's a first for everything,' he said. Davis didn't say anything. He pinched his nose and closed his eyes. He felt a pain gather in his ears and begin to spread into his brain. It was a regular pain; he knew its depths, and he understood its meaning. Its warning. He wasn't meant to be a policeman, he hadn't been born to walk this tide-line between scum and right. He was an animal lover, a man with a dog's mind and a cat's walk. He wanted out, and he wanted peace. When the car stopped at traffic lights, he opened his eyes and watched a shopper walking her dog along the street. He thought about his own dog, and about the Christmas present he was going to buy for it. He dreamed about early retirement and setting up a breeding kennel. Work and play, and all sleep in between.

The lights changed, Evans turned right and said, 'Would you say that he was a vindictive man?'

'I wouldn't have, but now...' Frank picked some loose skin from his thumb and dropped it on the floor, 'I don't know.'

'What's different about now?'

'Anyone who can kill his wife...'

'Who said anything about him killing her?'

'I thought...'

'Amateur,' said Davis.

'For all we know, it was you.'

'Me?'

'Why not? A beautiful woman, you go round to spin some yarn about Tai Chi, but she doesn't want to play your game. She decides honesty is the best policy, you don't agree. You argue, she insists, you lose your temper and before you know it...'

'I don't lose my temper.'

'No?' said Evans.

'Where were you last night between nine and half-one?' said the colleague.

'At home.'

'Can you prove that?'

'Yes.'

'Clever boy.'

'I was with my neighbour.'

'Name?'

Frank told him as Evans turned off the shopping street and drove down an avenue of semi-detached houses. 'Her boyfriend had left her; I was consoling her.'

'So you're a saint?'

'I didn't say that,' said Frank. He pointed to a house with a yellow door. 'The sister's.'

'You're not a saint?'

'I didn't say that either.'

'So what are you?'

'The sister?' said Frank.

The two policemen looked at the house, looked at Frank and looked at each other. A sparrow hopped along the pavement and flew away. The sky was small and flat, and its clouds were the size of coins.

'I think she left in a hurry,' said Evans. They were standing in the kitchen. Unwashed dishes were piled in the sink. The radio was on. Upstairs, clothes were strewn across the bedroom floor, and the smell of perfume was in the air.

Frank picked up a packet of cornflakes and shook it. 'Or else she's just untidy,' he said.

'You think so?'

'Why would she want to leave?'

'You tell me.'

'I don't know.'

'Fright?'

'I only met her once, but I don't think so.'

'Why not?'

'She frightened me.'

'You frighten easily, Frank?'

'No.'

'So you think she's gone to work as usual, ignorant of the fact that her girlfriend's lying in the morgue?'

'Maybe.' A cat wandered into the kitchen, looked at a bowl of food, sniffed it and began to eat. 'That's fresh.' He pointed at the cat food. 'If she was doing a runner, she wouldn't have bothered to feed the cat.'

'Don't you think so?' Evans turned to his colleague. 'You're an animal lover, sergeant; what would you do? Stop to spoon out the Whiskas?'

'Of course, Chief.' Davis winced, rubbed his forehead, and frowned. 'I wouldn't want to compound my guilt, as it were.' He bent down and stroked the cat.

Evans turned back to Frank and raised his eyebrows. 'Is she the guilty type?'

'Who knows?'

'Where does she work?'

'She's a teacher.'

'Is she?'

'Holy Oak. Design and Technology.'

'What's that?'

'They paint T-shirts, frig around with paint, you know.'

'I don't think I do,' said Evans, but I think I'm going to find out.' He put his hand on Frank's shoulder and squeezed. 'Maybe we could find out together.'

'Okay,' said Frank, 'why not?'

'Davis?'

Davis had his head against the cat's and was whispering to it.

'Davis?'

'Sir?'

'Come on.'

Davis stood up, the cat rubbed itself on his legs, he smiled at it and turned away.

The school secretary asked Frank, Evans and Davis to wait in the headmaster's office. Frank cleaned his nails, Evans studied a school photograph and Davis looked at the school goldfish. This fish was sick. It did the puckering thing with its lips, but couldn't suck the sodden gobs of food that floated around its bowl. Its scales had lost their shine, and its gills were shot; Davis flicked his fingers at the water, licked his lips and said, 'This fish is on the way out.'

'Want to call the RSPCA?' said Evans.

Davis shook his head, and a tiny ball of rage flared in his stomach. It bounced twice and found a hole that led to his gut. It slid sideways and dissolved. Fish had feelings. He took a deep breath and turned away. 'Too late.'

The door opened. 'Gentlemen.' The headmaster, a bald man with small feet, entered the room. 'What can I do for you?'

'Evans,' said Evans, and he flipped his card. 'We're looking for Diana Austin. She teaches here?'

'She does.'

'Could we have a word with her?'

'You could,' said the head, 'if she was here, but she called in sick this morning.'

'Sick?'

'Flu. There's a lot of it around.'

'I see.'

'Might I ask what this is about?'

'Routine enquiry,' said Evans. 'Some stolen property has turned up that we believe is hers. We have to check some details.'

'I see,' said the head.

'Thanks for your time,' said the sergeant.

'No problem,' said the head.

'Ideas?' said Evans.

'I've got to go to the office,' said Frank.

'Have you?' said Davis.

'You going to be there all day?'

'In and out,' said Frank.

'Don't go far.'

'Me?' said Frank.

'You,' said Davis.

'And you can tell your boss,' said Evans, 'Bob, isn't it?'

'Yes...'

'We'll want a word with him.'

'Okay...'

'Problem with that?'

'Maybe. He's been preoccupied.'

'With what?'

'Boredom, I think.'

'What's that?' said Evans.

Frank sat in the office, strung some paperclips together, stared out of the window for five minutes, wished he had shorter legs for another ten, then thought about killing people. Once, he had threatened to kill someone, but the thought had been miles from the action. What happens in a mind when it leaps from the thought to the deed? Is it something to do with chemicals surging, or electrical activity? Did Lisa want to kill Adrian, did Bob want to kill himself? Would Mrs Platt want to kill the vet if she knew the truth? What happens when people stop asking questions? Frank picked up a copy of *Yellow Pages* and turned to Garages. Lisa used to talk about meeting Adrian at Brakes and Tyres, or about going down there for lunch, or about getting a good deal at Brakes and Tyres on your brakes and tyres. He noted the address and went out.

Twenty minutes later, he was working a deceit on one of Adrian's old work-mates, John. Frank explained that he worked for the Valley Insurance Company, and had the cheque with him.

'What cheque?'

Frank took a blank envelope out of his pocket and waved it. 'Mr Coleman made a claim last month; he asked us to deliver the money personally.'

'But he doesn't work here any more. He left yesterday.'

'Can you tell me where he is?'

John had been made to swear to keep his mouth shut. Nobody must know, don't trust anyone, don't say a word. 'I can't,' said John.

'Can't or won't?' said Frank.

'I promised.'

'You promised.' Frank shook his head gravely. 'Good. But what's he going to say when he finds out, and he will, that you're responsible for him missing out on over two hundred pounds, two hundred pounds he claimed for, two hundred pounds that's rightfully his.'

John thought slowly.

'John?'

'I could send it to him.'

'You could not.'

John said, 'I should call him.'

'And tell him what? Sorry, but I'm screwing up your chance of getting a wad?'

John thought again, wiped his hands on a cloth and said, 'Wait here.' He came back two minutes later with a piece of paper. 'There,' he said. 'Dixon's Motors, Forth Street, Carlisle. I haven't got the number.'

'This is all I need,' said Frank. 'Thanks.' He reached into his pocket and pulled out a fiver. 'One more thing,' he said, pressing the note into John's hand, 'if he calls, don't say anything about this. We like our payments to come as a surprise to our customers.'

'Oh,' said John, blankly, 'okay.'

'Good man.'

John looked at the fiver and smiled. Frank left the garage and drove back to the office.

'Austin's turned up.' Evans's voice was flat and unhurried.

'What's his story?' Frank swopped the telephone receiver from one hand to the other.

'Good question; if I knew, I'd tell you, but he's proving difficult.'

'Where was he?'

'Down the front.'

'When did you find him?'

'This morning.'

'Did he do it?'

There was a pause before Evans said, 'I don't think so.'

'Can I talk to him?'

'It would be useful to us if you could,' said Evans. 'You can establish contact with the after-life?'

'What do you mean?'

'He's dead, Frank.'

'Dead?'

'Gone on...'

'How?'

'Drowned,' said Evans. 'We fished him out the drink an hour ago. He'd been dead about twelve hours.'

'I see.'

Evans coughed. 'I have to say, Frank, that you don't seem very surprised.'

'I'm shocked.'

'Or shocked.'

'Have you any idea who did it?'

'Did what?'

'Killed him?'

'Now, Frank, wait. I never said anything about murder. He was drowned, and at the moment, we're working on the assumption that he killed his wife, and then, in a fit of remorse, committed suicide. He was a big man, not very fit, the water was freezing. I doubt he could swim.' Evans tapped a piece of paper. 'He's got a mother. We gave her a call; she's coming from Canterbury.' He coughed again. 'Not that she'll be able to shed any light...'

'He could,' said Frank.

'What?'

'He could swim.'

'Really?'

59

'Yes.'

'How do you know?'

'I met him at The Pines.'

'The Pines?'

'The country club. He was in the pool when I arrived.'

'Swimming?'

'Breaststroke.'

Evans nodded, but didn't say anything. He was looking forward to Christmas. His three children and eight grand-children would be visiting. He loved children, he loved giving and receiving presents, he loved helping to decorate the house, and he loved singing carols door to door. He lived for happy, smiling faces standing at hollied doors, he breathed the smell of mince pies and cream. A glass of brandy, coins rattling in a tin, another house and another group of faces. Christmas was Evans's time. He had not been born to be a policeman, and sometimes, in his deeper moments, he thought he should have been born a woman. A feminine streak ran through his body and creased the folds of his skin. He didn't know exactly how, but he'd drifted into policing; one day he was looking for a career, the next it was 1973 and he was on the beat with another rookie. Ten years later he was being promoted, and then he had his own office with a view of Brighton's rooftops. He liked The Beatles, he read Dickens, and he sympathised with squatters. He enjoyed Indonesian food and smoked a cigar on his birthday.

'Hello?' said Frank.

'Yes?' said Evans.

'Were there any unusual marks on Austin's body?'

'What?'

'Marks. Wounds?'

'Are you trying to tell me my job?' Evans snapped.

'No. I just thought…'

'He was covered in fish bites,' said Evans, 'but we've ruled all forms of marine life out of the enquiry.' He smiled weakly. 'No motive.'

Frank phoned Bob and told him to meet him for a drink. Bob said that he was in the bath, and couldn't see him until the afternoon. Frank didn't try to persuade him to change his mind; instead, he went to see Lisa. He found her up a ladder, rearranging a shelf of perfume. He said, 'Be careful.'

'Yeah,' she said, without looking at him.

'When's your lunch hour?'

She glanced at her watch. 'Twenty minutes.'

'I'm buying,' he said.

'I'm not hungry.' Her mouth was dry and her head ached. The perfumes had fazed her nose and made her eyes water. Her feet ached and she felt giddy.

'You will be,' he said, and he left the shop and stood on the pavement to wait.

He walked up and down, he counted the number of cars he saw, and he watched children press their faces against the shop windows. The sound of carols drifted from open doors, and fairy lights blinked off and on. A decorated tree stood at the top of the street, its branches weighed down with gift-wrapped empty boxes. The smell of fried bacon wafted in the air, and chips. An old woman was having trouble crossing the road; an old man offered to help her. They crossed together, picking their way over the piles of slush that lined the gutters. A motor cyclist sped by, the back wheel of his bike threatening to slide sideways as he took the bend at the top of the street. A woman in a fur coat climbed into a taxi, leaving her shopping to be loaded by the driver. A bus stopped at traffic lights, and its passengers stared through its streaming windows, their faces lulled by the condensation so they looked liked blooming flowers on short stalks. A pair of seagulls spotted some open dustbins and flew down to peck at a plastic bag; Frank was watching them when Lisa came out.

'Hungry yet?' he said.

'No.' She held her stomach. 'I was terrible this morning.'

'You drank enough.'

'You should have stopped me. I wasn't thinking straight.'

'I didn't dare.'

'I'm sorry.'

'You're sorry!' He laughed.

She didn't. 'It's my problem. I shouldn't have gone on at you like that.'

'I didn't mind.'

'No,' she said, 'you didn't, did you?'

He shook his head. 'Besides,' he said, and he looked into her eyes, 'I know where he is.'

'Where who is?'

'Adrian. I know where he's gone.'

Lisa stared blankly. Frank watched her brain work. It flashed signals to her eyes, and her eyes showed no emotion. 'How?' she said.

He tapped the side of his nose. 'It's my job.'

Lisa continued to stare. 'Do I want to know?'

'I don't know.'

'I don't,' she said.

'Okay.'

'Where is he?'

'Lisa?' Frank snapped his fingers in front of her eyes, she blinked, licked her lips and shuffled her shoulders.

'Tell me,' she said. Now her eyes were swivelling, and she was wringing her hands.

'Are you sure you—'

She grabbed his arm and squeezed. 'Where is he?'

'Steady.'

'Tell me!'

Frank wrenched his arm away.

'Frank!'

He began to walk.

'Where are you going? Frank!'

He speeded up.

She caught him and grabbed his arm again. He brushed her off. 'Frank! Please! I don't need shit like that, but I've got to know. I want to…'

'Look!' He turned around. People were staring. 'Either we discuss this quietly, rationally, or we don't. Your Adrian isn't just another job to me, but he could be. I don't have to go around pretending I'm someone else just to keep you happy.'

'What are you talking about?'

'You want the truth, but I have to lie to get it.'

'Eh?'

People were still staring. 'Oh God,' he said. 'Come on. I'll tell you about it.'

Two hours later, Frank rang Bob again. Bob was listening to 'La Clemenza Di Tito' and watching television with the sound down. 'The more I hear your words, the greater grows my passion. When one soul unites with another, what joy a heart feels! Ah, eliminate from life, all that is not love!' He had a bowl of peanuts on his lap, and the remains of a newspaper covered his legs. He was thinking about the Romans, and he was thinking about having a long, hot bath. When the phone rang, he grabbed it and snapped, 'What?'

'Bob?'

'What is it, Frank?'

'We've got to talk.'

'Must we?'

'Yes.'

'Do we have to?'

'It's important.'

'*Si tronchi dalla vita,*' said Bob.

'What?'

'Nothing.'

Frank scratched his head. 'Can I come round?'

'No.'

'Then I'll meet you here.'

'Invite me to a party, Frank, and then I'll be happy to come out. Otherwise, forget it,' he said, and hung up.

Frank rang back immediately.

'What?'

'I'm inviting you to a party.'

'When.'

'Tonight. Downstairs from my place. You know Mrs Platt?'

'No.'

'You'll like her. Half-eight. Bring a bottle.'

'Or two?'

'Or two,' said Frank, and he hung up.

9

The vet had never seen anything like the scene in Mrs Platt's room. He had a sherry. Then he had to have another. He'd been feeling guilty about killing her bird; accepting her offer of a drink was a way to make amends. Show kindness and a caring nature, and offer sincere condolences; he hadn't expected what he found.

Joey lay on a bed of red satin, and a candle burned at his head. Mrs Platt had washed him and brushed his feathers. Other candles burned around the room, and trays of glasses and bottles twinkled in their light. Chopin crackled in the background. Frank was having to raise his voice to make himself understood by Bob. Lisa was inspecting paintings, china and porcelain, swinging between tears and rage, and nursing a glass of wine. Mrs Platt was wearing black and dabbing at her eyes with a tissue. The vet had tried to make his excuses once, but she insisted. 'You were his best friend,' she said. 'He'd have wanted you to stay.'

Now the guilt could not be avoided. It was burning him. He had to tell her. 'Mrs Platt,' he began.

'Another sherry?' she said.

He looked at his glass. 'I have to say something.'

'Please,' she said. 'For him.'

The vet looked at the woman and tried to smile. 'Maybe just one more, but I must tell you—'

'Ssh,' she said, and she put a finger to her lips.

Frank put his arm on Bob's shoulder and said, 'Mrs Austin.'

'Good woman,' said Bob. He was holding a bottle of whisky in one hand, and a full glass in the other.

'How can I put this...'

'Tell it straight, Frank.'

'Shall I?'

'Flannel at your peril.'

Frank cleared his throat. 'She's been murdered.'

Bob looked at the bottle. 'Murdered?'

Frank nodded. 'And this afternoon, old man Austin turned up floating off the pier.'

Bob looked at his glass. 'Drowned?'

'Yes.'

'Had he paid his bill?' Bob took a swig, swilled it around his mouth and swallowed.

'What?'

'The bill, Frank. What was it?'

'Screw the bill.'

'Now, now; that's not the sort of attitude that's going to take you far. If you want to run the agency, you'll have to change your way of thinking.'

'I don't want to run the agency.'

'I thought it was agreed.'

'Nothing was agreed!'

'But this morning, we—'

'Bob! Two people are dead! The police think we know something they don't, and if we don't get our story right, we could be in the shit!'

'What's to get right?' Bob put his hand on Frank's shoulder and spilt whisky down his back. 'Did you do it?'

'No.'

'Nor did I.' He spread his arms and raised his voice. 'Two innocents in a world of guilt!' The vet looked up. 'Don't worry!'

'Easy enough to say if you've spent the day in the bath.'

'The truth will hurt,' said Bob, 'even if you are innocent,' and he took another drink.

'Shit,' said Frank.

'And foul language will get you nowhere.'

'Fuck you.'

Bob turned and picked up a china tortoise. He began to examine it, fingering the pattern on its shell; Frank left him and walked across the room to join Lisa. She was holding a winebottle, and standing on her toes to look at a painting. This was of a sailing ship in a storm, a crowded lifeboat, an angry sky and waves the size of the ship. She was wearing a short skirt, a blue shirt buttoned to her throat and sling-backs. 'Is he all right?' she said.

'Drunk,' he said. 'Drunk and sad. The old brothers in arms.'

'I know them.'

Frank hung his head and rubbed his eyes.

'What about you?' she said.

'It's been a long day.'

'And I never thanked you, I'm sorry.'

'What for?'

She poured some wine into her glass and put the bottle on a shelf. 'Adrian.' She drank. 'He can go to hell. Leaving was the best thing he ever did.' She patted her stomach. 'We're stronger without him.'

'Mrs Platt?' The vet's guilt was building houses in his head, furnishing them with blood and crushed bones. Strings of lies dangled in front of his eyes. He wasn't meant to feel like this.

'Yes?'

'I have to tell you something.'

'What, dear?' Mrs Platt smiled.

The vet envied Joey. He looked at the bird. It had oozed fluid on to its satin bed. 'It's about Joey,' he said.

'What about him?'

'When he died...'

Mrs Platt looked at the vet's glass. 'Do you want another drink?' she said.

'He was suffering,' he said.

'I know.' She patted his arm. 'And you did everything you could.'

'I did more than that.'

'What do you mean?'

'I had to make a decision.'

'I'm sure you did, dear, and I'm sure it was the right one.'

'He could have gone on for days, but when I looked at him I decided that the kindest thing to do was to let him go.'

'And then he did…'

'I killed him, Mrs Platt.' He looked at the bird. 'I killed Joey.'

Mrs Platt followed the vet's eyes as the words dumped themselves in her head.

'I broke his neck.'

Mrs Platt was holding a wineglass; her hand tightened around it, her lips puckered and her tongue flicked out and back in. She looked at the vet, she looked at the floor and back at the vet, and then she crushed the glass. The stem fell to the floor, she screamed and held out her hand. Slivers of glass had embedded themselves in her fingers and palm, and blood was dripping to the floor. 'You killed him?'

The vet nodded.

'Murderer!' she yelled. 'Murderer! And then you come round here and drink my sherry!'

'He didn't feel a thing.'

'How do you know?' She lunged at him but Lisa jumped between them.

'Mrs Platt!'

'That man!' she screamed. 'He's evil!' Her hands were shaking, blood was dripping on to the carpet, and spit flew from her mouth.

'It was for the best,' said the vet, as Frank took his arm and tried to get him out of the room. 'I wouldn't have done it if I hadn't thought—'

'There!' Mrs Platt let go with a triumphant yelp. 'He didn't think! Frank!'

'What?'

'Leave him to me.'

'I think you'd better go,' Frank said to the vet. The man nodded, and grabbed his coat.

'What is it?' said Mrs Platt. 'An eye for an eye?' and she lunged again. This time, she slipped and fell on the floor. She snatched at the vet's ankle, he shook her off, got through the door and crossed the hall. 'I want him!'

'Mrs Platt!' said Lisa.

Bob filled his glass.

'Go!' said Frank.

The vet went.

10

Bob slept on Frank's sofa. He dreamt, but in the morning could not remember his dreams. They were like people in the street, hurrying to work. He saw them, then they were gone. They left clouds of mist that clotted and then faded into buildings. When he woke up, Frank had left for the office. There was a note on the table. 'Bob. Do you remember what I said last night? If you do, call me. If you don't, call me. Frank.' Bob went back to sleep.

Inspector Evans called Frank and asked him to come to the police station.

Frank looked at his legs. 'Now?' he said.

'Yes,' said Evans.

Frank looked at the cover of the Austin file, and at a stack of paper in a wire tray. Unpaid bills, letters of introduction and requests for information spilled out of it. 'I'll be there,' he said.

A fresh fall of snow had layered the slush, the roofs of cars and houses, and the branches of the squat trees that lined the pavement. Frank walked. Workmen were spreading grit from the back of a lorry, and an angry Father Christmas argued with a policeman, shaking his bell and stamping his feet. The festive lights shone through a murk of car exhausts and gently falling snow. Old men and women looked up at the weather and rattled their teeth, and children yelled at each other.

'Good of you to come.' Evans stood up and smiled, but didn't feel very well. He was beginning to trust Frank; he saw something of himself in the man, the man he would have become if he'd avoided family. He was glad he hadn't avoided family; his wife and children and his children's children gave his life life. 'Please,' he said, 'take a seat.'

'Thanks,' said Frank.

Evans sat down and scratched his head. 'Eastbourne called.' He picked up a sheet of paper and passed it across his desk. 'Austin's sister's dead.'

Frank read.

'I don't know,' said Evans. 'Austin kills his wife, then commits suicide. Filled with remorse, his sister throws herself off Beachy Head?'

Frank passed the paper back. 'Or Austin throws his sister off Beachy Head, cuts his wife's throat, gets drunk and slips off the end of the pier? How long had she been dead?'

'Twelve hours.'

Frank raised his eyebrows.

'Maybe fourteen.'

'How about Austin kills his wife, his sister kills him, she kills herself.'

Evans swivelled in his chair, put his hands behind his head and tipped back. 'Bob, isn't it?'

'My boss?'

'I haven't spoken to him.'

'You'd be wasting your time. These days he can barely remember his name.'

'That bad?' said Evans.

'Not so much bad as weird,' said Frank.

'Weird's the worst sort of bad. Where is he?'

'I left him at my place.'

'You drive.'

Mrs Platt tidied up. Joey remained on his stained satin pillow, his tiny legs clenched like pliers and all his feathers lank. Mrs

Platt picked up one bottle at a time and carried them to the kitchen. She stood them by the back door and stared outside. Then she opened this door and aired her rooms.

Frank and Evans arrived as she was stacking plates in the sink and running the taps. She didn't hear them. Evans climbed the stairs quickly, Frank loped behind him. He touched Lisa's door as he passed, then took the flight to his flat in three strides.

Bob had made himself a cup of coffee and was lying in the bath, drinking and reading a copy of H.G. Wells's *A Short History of the World*. When Frank and Evans walked in, he said, 'I've got a problem. Given that the speed of light is the fastest anything can travel, how did the universe expand from nothing to infinity in a nanosecond?'

'Bob?' said Evans.

'Who's your friend, Frank?'

'Evans.' He flipped his card. 'And I've got a problem too.'

'Then take a bath. I never really appreciated how good they could be for you, not just as a way of getting clean, but as a restorative.'

'Where were you last night?'

'Me?' Bob rubbed his chest with a bar of soap and looked at Frank. 'Frank?'

'He was with me,' said Frank. 'We were at a wake.'

'Anyone we know?' said Evans.

'Joey.'

'Joey who?'

'Joey the budgie.'

'The budgie?'

'Yes.'

'A budgie?'

Frank nodded.

'You went to a wake for a budgie?'

'Downstairs. It was my landlady's. Mrs Platt. She worshipped the bird. People get very attached to their pets; she treated it like a kid.'

'Tell me about it.' Evans shook his head. 'My sergeant's like that with his dog.'

'I hate dogs,' said Bob.

'You were at this wake all night?'

'Why?' said Bob. He squeezed his soap, and it flew out of his hand, crossed the bathroom, landed and skidded across the floor.

'Another Austin's dead.'

'Another?'

'The sister.'

'God,' said Bob. 'What's the matter with them?'

'I was hoping you'd be able to tell me,' said Evans.

'Me?' Bob shook his head. 'I haven't got a clue.'

'You don't seem very surprised.'

'Why should I be? The world's four and a half thousand million years old and you expect me to be surprised by three people dying? Tell me that they've turned into antelope and I'll be surprised; I might even get out of the bath for that, but death...' He stuck a finger in his right ear. 'Death's nothing. Happens every day.'

Evans looked at Frank and raised his eyes to the ceiling. 'Okay,' he said, and, 'Thanks,' and he left the bathroom.

Frank followed and said, 'Satisfied?'

'No,' said Evans, 'but I never am.'

The vet was distracted, he couldn't concentrate, he couldn't focus on a cat's bollocks and had to ask for a five-minute break. When he went back to the operation, the surgery nurse offered to make him a cup of tea.

'Thanks,' he said, 'but I'll be all right now.' He cut. 'I had too much to drink last night.'

The nurse tutted and passed him a swab.

The vet sliced, removed and stitched automatically. He thought about his girlfriend as he worked, the firm and beautiful Cheryl. Cheryl with perfect teeth, slim hips and hair like cotton. He kept Mrs Platt away by thinking about the time he had sneaked into the surgery where Cheryl had worked. The dentists had gone to a party, the receptionist had gone home to cook a meal; the place had been dark, empty and smelt of mint. Cheryl and he had used a dentist's chair to make love on, across, over, below, around, under and beside. He had been excited by the sterility of the place and thoughts of the germed fluids they were spreading, she had been juiced by the fear that a boss could walk in at any moment. Together, they made a lot of noise and tipped over trays of instruments; he smiled at the mess they left.

After the operation, he left the surgery and went for lunch. As he walked Rick Street, he continued to think about Cheryl. Her stomach, her thighs, her curly hair brushing against her cheeks, the sound of her voice and her laugh; all these things kept thoughts of the night before away. The clean taste of her mouth and her carefully trimmed fingernails; he stepped off the pavement and began to cross the road.

Two minutes earlier, Angela Switt had turned left into Rick Street, driven fifty yards and stopped at traffic lights. As she sat in the car, she drummed impatiently on the steering wheel and cursed her husband. At breakfast, he had told her that her plans to learn German were impractical, that she had never achieved anything and she wasn't going to change now. She had achieved a lot, but not on his terms. He was a blinkered man, he had no sense of humour, and he owned three fruit and vegetable shops. His world was filled by apples and bananas, courgettes and Kenyan beans; his wife and children were minor irritations. For five years, she had convinced herself that he would change; now the truth had dawned, and it was not meant to be. She had married the wrong man.

She remembered Ronald, her first love. As the lights changed, she accelerated down Rick Street and her mind filled with him. His love for her had overwhelmed her; its intensity had lit streets. She wondered where he was now, she wished that she had not thrown away his letters, she remembered the way his hair curled over his neck. When he moved to Manchester, why hadn't she pursued him? Why had she met her husband? How had her husband charmed her? Was Ronald still in Manchester? Could she find out where he lived? Was he married? Did he still taste of toffee? Did he ever think about her?

She pictured his face, and it filled her eyes. She was not driving down Rick Street in Brighton now, she was lying on a bed in Greece, and he was looking down at her. He was tanned and fit, and smelt of olives. A warm and gentle breeze rustled the curtains. There was a view from the window of scrubby hills, and beyond them, the sea. The sky was huge and blue, and the sun boiled sand. It was not Brighton and it was not snowing, she was not sitting in a muggy car with a crying child on the back seat. Garish lights did not hang between streetlamps, and morose shoppers did not stare at shop windows. Angela wanted to cry.

The vet didn't look and Angela did not see. One was think-ing about his girlfriend's perfect nails, the other could smell taramasalata in her car. Someone shouted 'Look out!' and another yelled 'Watch it!' The vet saw the car too late, Angela put her foot on the brakes, her wheels locked and she began to slide down the street sideways. He was clipped by the edge of the front bumper, then slammed by the driver's door. He began to rise into the air, and as he did, he screamed.

Angela saw his face, and it was a face she had dreamt of. It was full of regret and grief, and topped up with longing. All it wanted was life, but it knew it had no chance. It knew it was moments from death, and though it was not afraid, it was not calm. It was tinted with remorse, haunted by love and creased by memories it did not want to lose. It had not wasted its life, but it was too young to die. She heard her baby yelling behind her but she was transfixed by the image that passed in front of her. She noticed that the man was wearing red socks; as they passed by the window she thought that her husband had never owned a pair of red socks. Had this flying man bought the socks himself or had they been bought for him? Bought by the person he was haunted by, given to him in a carefully wrapped parcel; the car skidded to a halt as the vet landed on his head. Blood began to seep from his nose and stain the slush. He lay very still. A woman ran from a teashop shouting, 'Don't move him! I'm a doctor!' She knelt beside the vet but knew she could do nothing. One of his eyes was closed, the other stared at the sky. The doctor passed her hand over it, then removed her coat and laid it over his head. Then she stood and walked to the car; Angela was shaking and sobbing, and beating the steering wheel. 'Come on,' said the doctor. 'There's nothing we can do.' She leaned into the back of the car, unclipped the baby and cradled it in her arms. A crowd had gathered and was staring at the vet's body and pointing at Angela. The baby began to cry, and a police siren wailed in the distance. 'You need a cup of tea,' said the doctor.

Angela looked at the woman and shook her head. 'No,' she said. 'I need someone like the man I killed.'

'You didn't kill him.'

'I killed him,' said Angela, and she crashed her head against the steering wheel until blood filled her eyes.

11

Snow in Canterbury. Mrs Erica Austin sat in her kitchen, held her hands together in prayer, and waited for a taxi. The news of her children's deaths had shifted her mind, but had not penetrated. She had asked to be told the facts and the truth, but the policewoman who was sitting with her had apologised and said that she was unable to do that. 'I'm sorry. All I know is what I've already told you. My colleagues in Brighton will have the details...'

Mrs Austin nodded and said that she understood. She was seventy-one, and had worked as a nurse in the war. Wounded men had given her nylons and died, and she'd seen ten-year-old children hold oranges for the first time in their lives. Her husband had been a banker, and a frustrated opera singer. She had never been frustrated; she was a devout Christian, and believed that Christ's mercy could be seen in affliction and tragedy. She had never worn make-up, and she had never owned an umbrella. She used to drive a car, but stopped in 1975, after she reversed into a lamppost that should not have been where it was. Her hair was thick and wiry, and she loved Danish pastries. The taxi arrived, and the driver honked his horn.

'Mrs Austin?' said the policewoman.

'Yes?' She'd been thinking about the Tibetan custom of laying corpses on rocks for vultures to eat. Death as a window to the sky, as a way of flying. Death, life's widow. 'Remember, O Lord, what is come upon us.'

'Taxi's here.'

'Thank you.'

'Shall I take your bag?'

'No.' Mrs Austin stood up. 'I can manage.'

'Okay.'

The two women left the house, and as they walked down the front path, the policewoman said, 'Are you sure you don't want to be met in Brighton?'

Mrs Austin raised her voice. 'No!' she said. 'I can cope!'

'I'm sorry...' The policewoman stared at the ground, and felt tears behind her eyes. The taxi-driver stepped forward and took the bag. Mrs Austin shook her head. 'No,' she said, 'I'm sorry,' and she touched the woman's arm. 'I didn't mean to shout.' She dredged a smile. 'Bless you,' she whispered, and she left.

Lisa sat alone at a corner table. A man at the bar looked across at her, smoothed his hair and smiled; she sneered back and gave him the finger. He shrugged and turned back to his drink. She stared into hers, and as she did, she felt her embryo scratch. This felt as though it had travelled a great distance to be with her, and that hospitality was not enough. It was accompanied by a twinge that snapped at her spine and moved slowly towards her neck. Her focus faded, her drink swam across the table, she closed her eyes and pinched her nose. She took a breath, and when she opened her eyes again, the feeling had gone, and she felt calm.

Sergeant Davis was walking his dog along the front. Nothing gave him more pleasure; away from the station, forgetting the scum he had to deal with, giving himself a break. The sea rustled the beach, the sky was drifting with a light curtain of snow, the air was clean and cold. His dog, a Yorkshire terrier, was his closest friend, his confidant and the reason he looked forward to going home every evening. Chips was a snappy, barky little bastard, a spoilt bundle of neuroses, a dog that trusted no one but its master, who nipped at strangers for no other reason than spite. It was overfed, indulged and given a bath every Thursday.

Davis was a loner, a man whose ambition had stopped in 1991; he was happy to be a sergeant. Responsibility scared him. Relationships confused him, he didn't know how to talk to women, and he didn't think that children were people. He could remember some details of his own childhood, but he preferred not to. His parents had been Christians who hit him for looking at them the wrong way. They had brought him up to believe that music stopped with Mozart, and that literature was a dangerous nonsense. Emotion had been frowned on by his father; Davis had never seen the man kiss his mother, or shout at her. Opinions had been forbidden, argument had been forbidden, sex could never become a hobby, entertainment had to be earnt. Homosexuality was a disease that could be cured by prayer. Jazz was a sin. Life in the Davis house was lived on the top deck of a superficial bus that cruised the suburbs of a world that ignored itself. When he got off to become a policeman, he never looked back. He bought a dog for company and called him Chips. Dogs could be trusted to trust him, they didn't answer back and were always grateful.

Chips had come from a kennel outside Lewes, where the pedigree stretched back years, and rosettes covered the feeding-room walls. The air had been filled with the sound of yapping, and the owner of the place had been Davis's type of person. A shy, monosyllabic woman with huge eyebrows and a beard; she had shown him the new litters, then left him to make his mind up. There had been no pressure and no fuss; Davis had stood and waited for the right pair of eyes to fix on his. He'd known which dog would be his immediately; he and Chips had made an instant connection, and had filled each other's hearts with comfort. Happiness had written its name in the sky, and moved across the duck pond behind the kennels. 'I'd like that one,' he'd said, and Chips had known. He'd stuck his little ears up, and run his tongue over his teeth.

'Isn't he sweet?' said the kennel owner.

Davis agreed. He was full of the idea of companionship, of owning a dog that would obey him, that would depend and rely on him. 'Yes,' he said, and the woman opened the cage and picked the animal out.

Now, seven years later, the prosaic ideas had been added to; he had a deep, unconditional love for Chips, full of worry and care, constant thought and consideration. He fed the dog on choice cuts of meat, crunchy biscuits and freely available fresh water. He had bought him a pillowed basket to sleep in, and a variety of squeaky toys to play with. A duck, a rubber biscuit and an orange ball. The television would be turned off when programmes the dog found disagreeable were shown, and they'd play instead, or go for a walk. Chips liked to walk, he liked to linger at smells, and Davis was a patient waiter.

The cold had killed all but the strongest smells; Davis walked quickly, and only stopped a few times to allow Chips to linger. He pressed the button on its retractable lead, and allowed the dog the freedom to roam a bit.

Mrs Platt heard about the vet on the local television news. She had been in the kitchen making a pot of tea, and glanced up to see his face on the screen. At the time, she'd still been simmering with hatred for the man, and her first reaction had been to spit, but then she heard the newsreader explain that it had been a tragic accident, the second of the week that could be blamed on the cold weather. A council official was grilled about the lack of grit on the roads and pavements; he claimed that they were spreading as much as they normally did, under the circumstances. 'What circumstances?' asked the reporter. 'Winter,' said the official.

Mrs Platt sat down. Her last words to the vet came back to her, and she wondered if they had rung in his ears as he died. She hadn't meant them. They'd been said through a haze of fury. He hadn't been an evil man, he'd believed that he was doing the right thing. She understood that now. Mrs Platt had always tried to understand the other person's point of view; what had enraged her was his deceit, the fact that he hadn't told her at the time. He hadn't been a murderer, she didn't believe in retribution. She saw the scene of the accident, a coned spot in Rick Street, the curious shoppers and a policeman with a grim face and folded arms. An interview with the doctor who covered his face with her coat, and a shot of the outside of the veterinary surgery. Then the news moved on to a piece about Brighton and Hove Albion FC, and Mrs Platt turned it off.

She sat in front of the blank screen for ten minutes, then stood up and went back to the kitchen. She poured a cup of tea, leant on the sink, stared at the night and felt guilt creep up to her. To begin with, it just tweaked her ears, but then it began to whisper. It suggested that she was responsible, that her anger had upset him so much that he'd become preoccupied with it, had been feeling guilt too, had not been able to concentrate all day, had crossed the road without thinking, had died with a head full of regret. A young man, bleeding in the road with a girlfriend wearing a silver ring he had bought her waiting for him somewhere; the night that blurred the world came to her kitchen window and tapped on the glass. When she heard Frank come in, she turned and hurried to her front door, opened it and blurted, 'The vet's dead!'

'What?' said Frank.

'The vet,' she said. 'He was knocked down by a car. Killed. This afternoon...'

'Your vet?'

Mrs Platt nodded, and she began to cry.

Frank's head was overloaded with deaths; another bounced against the others and barely bruised them. He put his arm on her shoulder and led her back into her rooms, and sat next to her on a tassled couch. 'Are you sure?' he said.

She waved a finger in the direction of the television. 'It was on the news.'

Frank struggled for the words, and came up with 'Accidents —' a pause, 'happen,' and immediately regretted them. They acted like a pantomime horse on ice. They had the grace of blood and the poise of nothing. 'I'm sorry,' he mumbled.

Mrs Platt shook her head. 'Don't,' she whispered, 'don't be.' She sniffed and rummaged in her sleeve for a handkerchief. 'Mr Platt used to say "I'm sorry," all the time, and I hated it. He'd say it —' and she paused to blow her nose, 'if he hit his thumb with a hammer.'

Frank smiled, but not broadly. He was beginning to wonder if he'd ever do anything broadly again, and he was beginning to feel very tired.

'You never met Mr Platt, did you?'

'No,' said Frank.

'That's a pity. He was a lovely man.' She nodded at his memory. 'He used to bring me a present every Friday.'

'He loved you.'

'He did,' said Mrs Platt. 'He loved me so much. When he died I could still feel his love all around. It's faded now, but it's still there. Here.' Her eyes widened, and she concentrated on a distant spot in the room. 'Like now,' she said, 'it's here now.' She wiped her nose and tucked the handkerchief away. 'Love is stronger than death, isn't it?'

Frank nodded, but he didn't say anything, because he wasn't sure what the answer should be.

* * *

The cold had not killed a smell that lingered at a bus stop. Chips caught it and stopped, and began to sniff madly. It was of metal and prunes, piss and leather, plastic and bananas, grit and water. There was hair and meat there too, and a hint of rabbit. Sergeant Davis let Chips have the entire length of the lead, and watched the dog for a moment before spotting an advertisement in a travel agency window. He went to take a closer look, and as he did, had to stand with the lead at a right angle around the corner of the shop door. Chips was out of sight.

Winter holidays were available in many countries. There was a trip to Lapland by Concorde, a ten-day break in Jamaica and a fortnight in Malta. These were just some of the bargains on offer; more were posted on a board inside the shop, over a desk.

Davis remembered the last holiday he had taken, in the lonely days before Chips. He had spent a week in Scotland, where he had been bitten to death by midges and deafened by bagpipe music in a restaurant. He'd tried to enjoy himself but found it impossible; something had been missing from his life, but at that time he hadn't known what.

Something had been missing from Bob's life, and now he knew what it was. As he sat in the sauna at The Pines Country Club, he sat back, narrowed his eyes and let the heat cover him, fill him and turn him glossy. He leaned forward and tossed a ladle of water on to the hot rocks, and watched the steam rise. Nothing reminded him of Frank or the agency, or the events that were knotting themselves around Brighton. He was calm and his pores were humming to each other.

He had seen advertisements for saunas you could have in your own home; they took up less room than a wardrobe, and could be fitted anywhere. Then, the intense cleaning experience, the healing heat of your own personal cabin could begin to transform your life; Bob knew it, and wondered why it had taken him so long to realise that this was it, that this was bliss. To sit naked in a streaming twilight of heat, a heat that stole every thought you ever had and rendered it impotent, a twilight of constant orange and pine. The smell of resin and steam. Bob knew that life was too short for dithering, and concluded that the Finns had stumbled on a verity. He leant back and watched a stream of sweat cascade off his forehead and run down his chest, and then he closed his eyes.

Mrs Austin sat on the train and stared at the night through her reflection. Moonlight shone on the fields of Kent. Tears filled her eyes though she had not been expecting them, and they tumbled and pooled on the floor. Another passenger rustled his newspaper and tried not to look, but when she took a deep breath and let out a long involuntary moan, he leaned forward and said, 'I'm sorry, but are you all right?'

Mrs Austin looked at the man. He was dressed in a pin-stripe suit, white shirt and tie, and black brogues. He had put a care-fully folded coat in the luggage rack, and a plain briefcase on the floor.

'No,' she said, 'not really.'

He reached into his pocket and pulled out a handkerchief. He offered it. 'It's clean,' he said.

She looked at it, took it, pressed it to her face and mumbled, 'My children are dead.'

The man cupped a hand over an ear and said, 'I'm sorry?'

Mrs Austin crushed the handkerchief and looked up. 'Cyril and Diana,' she said.

'Who are they?'

'My son and daughter.'

'And you're going to visit them?'

'They're dead,' she said.

The man dropped his newspaper. The pages floated across the carriage like greying feathers from hell. 'God,' he said. 'I'm sorry.' The words dropped like stones.

'I don't know how, I don't know why.'

The man tried to think of something else to say, but his head was jammed.

'I don't even think I believe it. Maybe they'll be waiting for me at the station.'

The man looked up. 'Yes,' he said, hopefully. 'I expect there's been a mix-up.' He reached out and began to gather up the pages of his newspaper. 'It happens all the time.'

'Does it?' said Mrs Austin.

'Oh yes,' said the man.

Mrs Austin nodded, and though she wished and wished, she knew that what she had been told was the truth, and the truth wore weeds.

Chips stepped off the pavement and began to sniff some slush in the gutter. There was piss and fish in it, and as he nuzzled his nose into the smell, a bus approached. A woman put her hand out to stop it, the driver flipped down a gear, checked his rear-view mirror and touched the brakes. He was tired and looking forward to going home. He was a young man, married with three children. He did not see Chips, and as the front near-side wheel ran over the animal, he didn't feel the impact. Passengers on the bus didn't see anything, and people waiting to climb aboard were too busy to notice; life left the dog without a whisper or a look, and left the corpse as flat as a board. Davis continued to read the adverts in the travel agency's window as the bus pulled away, then pulled on the lead and whistled. When there was no reaction, he turned the corner and saw the back of a disappearing bus, and his dog in the road. From where he was standing, it didn't look dead. Davis whistled again, and then pressed the button that reeled the lead on to its spool.

The dog moved a few inches, then caught the kerb. Davis tugged and narrowed his eyes. It was only when a pedestrian screamed and another shouted at the bus that he realised something was wrong. He ran, the lead whipped into its spool, he dropped it and saw Chips oozing now, his guts in his mouth and his feet splayed at bad angles. He heard someone shout, 'It was the bus!', he twitched, shut his eyes quickly, then opened them again. Chips was still dead, Chips was flat. In his life, Davis had seen women with their throats cut and men with air where their brains should have been, and these sights had not put him off bacon, but this was too much for him. He dropped the lead and tipped his head back, opened his mouth and let out a cry that started in his feet and shot through his body like a bullet. It filled the air, and made children run in fright. He wailed and howled, he dropped to his knees and tried to pick the dog up. An eyeball dropped out of Chips's ear and lay on the pavement. Davis picked it up and put it in his pocket, then sat down and cradled the animal in his arms. He rocked backwards and forwards, tears ran down his face, the Brighton night filled with his keening, and all the blame in the world sat upon his shoulders.

12

Inspector Evans was eating his dinner. His wife was telling him that it was time he got the Christmas-tree lights out of the attic. 'You know what'll happen. You'll find a couple of broken bulbs, but by the time you get down to the shops, they'll have sold out.'

'They don't sell out of them,' he said. He was enjoying a potato.

'They did last year,' said his wife, 'and don't talk with your mouth full.'

Inspector Evans shook his head.

'And don't shake your head like that.'

'How would you like me to shake it?' he said.

Mrs Evans, who liked a bit of a spat, smiled at her husband. He reminded her of her children, and that reminded her of her grandchildren, and then she thought about Christmas and got a warm feeling. She leaned across the table, reached out and stroked the back of his hand. He did not flinch.

'I'll get them down later,' he said.

'Thank you, dear.'

'Now, can I finish my dinner?'

'Of course you can.'

'Thanks.' He cut a piece of fish and put it in his mouth.

'Did you have a bad day at work?'

'Why?' It was haddock.

'I just wondered,' she said. 'I like to know these things.'

Inspector Evans looked at his wife as if he'd just met her. Sometimes she amazed him. Sometimes she bled questions, other times she said little and meant less. Christmas made her and snow gave her purpose. Winter was her drug, and all the things she wanted.

Frank left Mrs Platt and went upstairs. He took a bottle of Volvic from the fridge, pulled a chair to the window and sat down.

He sipped his water and watched the street. A light went on in the house opposite, and he saw the shadow of a woman climb a wall, cross a ceiling and then disappear. Frank waited a minute, swilling the bottle and wondering whether to phone Bob, when the shadow returned and turned on a television. A car drove down the street, and a dog began to bark. The woman opposite closed her curtains and her shadow faded. It went like paper in a fire, twisting and then floating into the air. It could have whispered and it could have sighed; Frank heard nothing, and cared less.

He sat for ten minutes before Lisa came up and knocked on his door; he let her in and offered her a cup of coffee. She looked pale, and her eyes were filmed and red. As he fiddled with the kettle she stood by the window, hugged herself, took a deep breath and said, 'Have you seen Mrs Platt?'

'Half an hour ago,' he said. 'She'd had a shock.'

'What?' She moved from the window, sat in an easy chair and wiped the palms of her hands.

'Her vet was killed.'

'Her what?'

'The vet. He was at the party. You remember. She ended up shouting at him, telling him—'

'He's dead?'

'Yes.'

'How?'

'He was knocked down by a car.' Frank took a bottle of milk from the fridge. 'It was nothing to do with her, but she thinks that somehow it's her fault.' The kettle boiled. 'Something she said to him…' He spooned coffee into the mugs, poured the water and stirred.

'She *was* angry.'

'Anger doesn't kill people.' He carried the drinks from the kitchen, put them on the table and sat down.

'True,' said Lisa, and she put her hand on her stomach. Now, her baby flipped in her womb, calculated the sharpness of one knife and began to rage. It began to seethe, and her head began to churn, and all her wishes collided.

'You okay?'

Lisa nodded, then folded in her chair. 'No,' she whispered.

'What's the matter?'

'If this is being pregnant…' she took another deep breath, 'I don't want it.'

'Hey,' said Frank, and he moved to the edge of his chair and took her hand. It was too hot. 'You're boiling.'

'I know.'

'Have you got a temperature?'

She nodded again.

'Is it cramps?'

'Been reading your book again, Frank?'

'Don't mock.'

'I wasn't. I was…'

'Just don't.' She looked at him, then at the floor, then back at him. She put her hand on her belly again, and doubled up. 'Don't…'

'Have you seen a doctor?'

'No…'

'What's his name?'

'Her. Dr Stewart.'

'I'm going to call her.'

'No you're not.' She winced again, and tears flicked into the corners of her eyes.

Frank stood up and went to the phone.

'Frank!'

'What's her number?'

'Please…'

'Lisa?'

Her womb was beginning to burn, and her tubes were filling with smoke. When she swallowed, razor-blades gathered in her throat and skimmed her skin. They danced and nicked, and all she wanted was a glass of water. She said, 'I want a glass of water.'

Frank was thumbing the telephone directory; he found Dr Stewart's number and began to phone. 'What?' he said.

'Water.'

'In a minute.'

'No!' Lisa cried, and she tried to stand. She pushed herself out of the easy chair but her legs would not hold her. They felt her weight and gave up. She fell towards Frank, grabbed at his waist and slipped. He dropped the phone, caught her shoulders and lifted her back towards the chair. 'Water,' she said again, and he reached for the Volvic. He unscrewed the cap and she grabbed the bottle. She drank hungrily, spilling as much as she swallowed. Frank went back to the phone, and this time she did not try to stop him. The fire was stifled, her tubes rested and when she closed her eyes she did not feel her body run with agony. Frank's soft voice was somewhere close, but she could not tell what he was saying. Her baby smiled to itself, its fluid simmered and all its embryonic desires quietened for the night.

Ten miles away, on the other side of town, Cheryl lay on her bed and stared at a blank wall. Her face was dying, she was crying, and every minute passed like an hour. She had never said goodbye to him, she had not had the chance to tell him that she was ready to marry him, she had not told him that yes, she would love him to cover her breasts with *fromage frais,* she would love to go to Australia with him, she wanted to do a bungey jump, she didn't mind seeing that film last week, she would remember not to floss in public. She wanted to be a vet's wife, she wanted to live with a small number of stray animals, she wanted to get used to cat hair, she wanted to go for long walks with old spaniels, she wanted to leave the world of teeth behind. Except his teeth, his teeth were beautiful, his teeth were perfect, his teeth were his. She pulled another tissue from the box and held it to her eyes. All the sadness in the world was crowding around her face, muttering words she couldn't catch. There was pain in the air, and it was playing like a child on a swing. She would never have his babies, she would never feel his fingers toying with her hair again, or taste his breath on hers. Death is final, death is the present grief gives itself. Cheryl turned over and faced the opposite wall, she closed her eyes and tried to fade away.

Ten miles away, in a different part of town, Sergeant Davis stood in his frozen garden. He had dug a hole beneath a cracked apple tree, and now, as he cradled Chips in a damp blanket, he tried to cry. He forced blame, did some origami with guilt and raged against himself. The dog's blood seeped through the blanket and covered his hands; he felt cold and he felt hot, and as he bent to lay Chips in the ground, his knees cracked.

He wondered how he had come so far and reached so little. His days were filled with rot, the fag-ends of humanity, the cries of blameless victims and the desperation of people who could not help themselves. People like the person who had killed Chips, people like the person who had cut the young Mrs Austin's throat, people like Austin, who had had the right idea. He had drowned himself and not looked back. As he stared at Chips, Davis wondered what was most difficult; the dying or the not looking back. Was it possible that as you died you could look forward? Is this what faith was about, or was faith an individual's construct, no faith the same as the next? His parents had claimed that they were Christians; as Christian as anyone else who thought they were. They had not been imaginative people; when he had misbehaved, their beliefs had encouraged them to beat him, and convinced them that they should send him to a school that beat him. He grew up thinking that punishment was Christianity's laugh, that pain was Christ's gift to the world, that God enjoyed the sound of wailing and the sight of blood. Whatever; without bothering to invent an excuse, Sergeant Davis said a prayer over his dog's grave, then filled it and went indoors.

Dr Stewart saw Lisa in Frank's flat at half-past ten, and immediately phoned for an ambulance. At this time, the patient was lying on the floor clutching a hot-water bottle to her stomach, wrapped in blankets. She was shivering, and every breath she took scorched her throat. Frank was pale and fussing, close to panic before the doctor arrived, who recognised the symptoms. 'What is it?' he said.

Dr Stewart, a short, brusque woman with short, grey hair, gave him a quizzical look and said, 'Are you the father?'

'Of course I'm not the bloody father!' he said. 'I'm just her friend. She lives downstairs.'

'I'm sorry. I didn't mean to...'

'What's the matter with her?' Frank hardly recognised his own voice; it tumbled and fell out of his mouth in alarm, dropped to the floor and slithered around.

'I can't be certain.'

'Yes, you can. It's in your eyes.'

Dr Stewart turned and looked at Lisa, who opened her eyes and said, 'Yeah, I'm still here.'

'Later,' said the doctor. 'Maybe you should go downstairs and wait for the ambulance.'

Frank nodded, went to Lisa, bent down and opened his mouth to speak, but Lisa put her fingers to his lips and said, 'No. Just do as she says.'

'I want to help you.'

'You've done enough.'

'Lisa...' Frank knew what he wanted to tell her, but fear held him back. All he could do was cradle her cheek in the palm of his hand, feel the pulse of blood through her body and wish a cure into the world. But the more he wished the more he felt that the world was killing, and that there was nothing he could do about it. And this was the only truth; there was nothing Frank could do, and nothing Lisa could hope for as the ambulance wailed to a stop in the street outside Mrs Platt's house.

13

Frank watched the dawn rise, its face showing over the houses opposite, through the trees on the distant downs, and in the cries of the gulls that gathered to scavenge the frozen bins. He watched it from his bed; when the alarm went, he slapped it off, got up, and stood in front of the window. Something about the day, something about the way it smelt filled him with a positive charge. It was in the heady gift it could give, and in the passion of the frozen birds that lined up on the telegraph wires and sung. Daylight and snow, business and play; Frank felt that he had to take charge. Things had to be put right. He had to take control. There were things he had to do, people to see and people to call. He washed in cold water, dressed quickly, drank a glass of orange juice and went downstairs.

Mrs Platt grabbed him before he could get outside, and said, 'Frank?' Frank, fired by resolve and purpose, was almost through the street door, but the old woman insisted. She did not let go until he stopped; then she said, 'Do you believe in reincarnation?'

'Mrs Platt...'

'Do you?'

Frank thought fast. 'Yes,' he said.

'Do you mean that?' she said.

Frank considered his positive charge, and decided that honesty was the foundation of this charge. He took Mrs Platt's hand and shook his head. 'I'm sorry,' he said. 'No. I don't mean it and I don't believe in reincarnation.'

'You should,' she said. 'A good man like you; you're the type who comes back better every time. With any luck, you might even come back as a bird.'

'I don't want to come back as a bird.'

'You wouldn't say that if you were a bird.'

Frank looked at Mrs Platt and decided to leave her where she was. She was deliberately undermining his resolve, as if his determination was something that could be so easily brushed aside. He laughed and said, 'No, I suppose I wouldn't,' and he pushed the street door open, and stepped outside. Mrs Platt watched him go, then returned to her rooms, her candles, the corpse of her dead bird and the smell of rot.

Lisa lay in her hospital bed, plugged into three machines. Tubes had been stuffed up her, and every kind of measurement had been taken. The diagnosis was a secret, the prognosis was unknown; the patient was uncomfortable but stable, and Frank was allowed to see her for five minutes, but then he would be asked to leave. The nurses ran a tight ship, and all who sailed in it wore disposable plastic aprons that rustled in the night.

Frank sat beside Lisa and held her hand. She had the glassy look that very sick people develop, the one that sheens their skin and gives their lips a purple tint. Her eyes were flecked with black spots, and her ears looked bigger than they really were. He said, 'Don't worry about that game of squash.'

'What game of squash?'

He shook his head.

'Did you bring me in?'

'No.'

'Who did?'

'An ambulance.'

'Have they said anything?'

'The doctors?'

'Yeah.'

'Not to me,' said Frank. 'What about you?'

Lisa shook her head. 'They smile like doctors do, and I've seen them talking to the nurses about me, but that's all. I suppose the only thing you can do is trust them.'

Frank agreed. He looked up at the three machines, and eyed their screens as they listened, watched and felt. One kept up a steady beep, the next held a steady gaze, the third held Lisa with a plastic pipe, and it would not let her go. 'Do you feel…' he had to rummage through his head, but it didn't help, 'any better?' The worlds sounded foolish, stripped bare by the antiseptic of the place.

'Than what?'

Frank shrugged. He wanted to lean forward and brush her curls off her cheek, but he was scared of the machines. As they worked, they flowed with the power of healing; he did not dare disturb their work or the careful display they made with tubes, screens, beeps, wires and electricity. He got as far as stroking the underside of her left forearm, but then he stood up, brushed imagined dirt from the front of his coat and said, 'Well…'

'Well, what?'

'I've got to see a man about a dog.'

'Okay.'

'I'll come again. Tonight?'

'I'd like that.'

'Would you?'

Lisa lifted her hand and wagged a finger at him. 'Don't be silly, Frank. You know I would.'

He almost kissed her then, but he turned instead and walked off the ward without looking back.

* * *

Bob woke late. It was ten o'clock. He sat upright, stared out of the window and then lay down again. He stretched and turned the radio on. A woman was talking about the Second World War, and how difficult life had been. The not knowing, the fear, the hunger, the noise of air-raid sirens. Bob lobbed a perfect shoe at the radio. It clattered to the floor and fell silent. He got up and went to the bathroom.

He loved his bed and he loved his bath, but now was not the time for either. Now was the time for action. He shaved carefully and he brushed his teeth with a brand new toothbrush. He padded to his wardrobe and chose a pair of cream slacks, a white shirt and a tweed jacket. He picked up Page and Bush's sauna catalogue and went to make some mushrooms on toast.

Bob's recipe for mushrooms on toast. Take a cast-iron skillet, warm it over a fierce heat, melt a knob of butter the size of a baby's fist, skim the scum. Add finely sliced (not chopped) mushrooms, and allow them to cook for two minutes. Add a teaspoon of German mustard, some freshly grated nutmeg, a pinch of salt and a twist of ground black pepper, toss the lot once, then serve on to previously prepared slices of hot buttered toast. Easy and delicious.

Bob ate slowly with the sauna catalogue propped in front of him, and he made a few mental notes. Did Page and Bush make a bottled-gas-fired model? Once a sauna was installed, was it possible to disassemble and re-erect it somewhere else?

Frank had some calls to make. First there was Bob.

'Bob?'

'Frank?'

'Are you coming in today?'

'What?'

'Are you?'

'Where? To the office?'

'No,' said Frank, 'to the cinema.'

'Why? What's on?'

'Bob?'

'Frank?'

'I was being ironic.'

'Oh,' said Bob, 'irony. Yeah.' He paused to think. 'And yeah, I am coming to the office today. Should I make an appointment or can I just turn up at any time? I wouldn't want to get in your way.'

'You won't.'

'Oh good.'

'We've got to talk.'

'Talk's cheap,' said Bob. 'Why don't we sing instead?'

Frank looked at the phone and thought about hanging up. He weighed the pros and cons; this took him five seconds. The pros did not exist, the cons were the size of buildings. He hung up. He waited another five seconds, then phoned 192.

'Directory enquiries. Which town please?'

'Carlisle.'

'Name of the people?'

'Dixon's Motors. Forth Street…'

The line cleared for a moment, then an automated voice gave Frank the number. Half a minute later he was asking to speak to Adrian Coleman.

'The new lad?'

'That's him,' said Frank.

'Hang on.'

Pause.

'Yeah?'

'Adrian?'

'Yeah. Who's this?'

'My name's Frank, you don't know me, but I'm a friend of Lisa's, and I thought you ought to know that she's—'

Adrian hung up.

Frank looked at the buzzing receiver and, for a moment, he thought that it was looking at him. Could inanimate objects generate a life of their own? Could they feel, could they understand? Could they watch you? Why was the telephone listening to him? He put it down, stood up and went to make himself a cup of tea.

As he waited for the kettle to boil, he stared down at the street, and watched a student dressed as a snowman smoke a cigarette. He had propped a sign against a wall: 'BUY REY-NOLD'S CAKES'. As he smoked, he dropped some ash on his costume, and when he tried to brush it off, he made a streaky mark. He threw the cigarette down, stamped on it, picked up a handful of snow and rubbed it on to the mark. Now the mark was a dirty smudge, impossible to miss. He thought about how angry Mr Reynold would be; it was a nightmare. Working as a snowman was a perfect holiday job. You were outside and you were warm. You could see what was going on, you got all the cakes you could eat. He tried some more snow, then he tried a handkerchief; it was no good. Finally, he started pulling at the mark, plucking pieces of material from the costume. He threw these pieces away; they were picked up by the wind and blown down the street. As they drifted into the sky they were joined by flakes of snow; after a few minutes, the man had got rid of the smudge, but a hole had appeared in its place. He tipped his head back and cursed as the kettle boiled in the office. Frank made the tea and carried his cup to the desk. He sat down, sipped and thought about Janet Black.

Janet Black had been nothing like Lisa; she had come from a rich family, but liked to slum it with people like Frank and Ray Butts, the butt bastard of every seaside town in England. Frank remembered playing strip poker with her; she had invented her own rules. These were based on ten even numbers she had written on her fingernails. You removed an article of clothing at the loss of a hand, and an additional forfeit was payable on the choice of a finger. It was a complicated game but typical of Janet, who fucked like an Easter bunny and now works at a composite signals station on the Devon/Somerset border that's not marked on any map.

Janet Black wore two of everything, so by the time Frank was down to his pants, she was still fully clothed. This, too, was typical of Janet, who was a deceitful woman with a nasty laugh and small eyes. But Frank was hooked. Her teeth, her fingers, her feet and her way of walking along the front. She didn't feel the cold and she didn't say thank you when he bought her a drink. That drove him wild. He had to have her, he had to show her what a man could do for a woman. His head flamed and when he looked at her his heart filled with a fatal longing. One day she told him that she loved a man in leather boots, so he spent his savings on a pair of boots that pinched from the day he bought them. But they were hand-tooled, had pointed toes and high heels, and they clicked when he walked; as he'd stood in a bar that night and ordered expensive drinks, Janet Black had stared at his boots and licked her lips. She is mine, Frank said to himself, and she will never regret the day.

Sergeant Davis didn't go to work. He hadn't slept, he couldn't eat, he hadn't opened his curtains, he hadn't answered the phone, he hadn't collected the paper or the letters from the mat, he hadn't gone to the bathroom, he hadn't left his bed, he hadn't closed his eyes, he hadn't thrown Chips's pillowed bed away, he hadn't stopped thinking about bus-drivers and how evil they were, he hadn't stopped blaming himself for the selfish way he'd looked in the travel agency's window, he hadn't stopped wishing he'd never bought a retractable fifteen-foot lead. What had been wrong with the old lead? Nothing had been wrong with the old lead. It had been as old as Chips, leather, with a silvered clip. Chips would sit up at the sound of its tinkly rattle, he would look at Davis with his big eyes, pleading for the walk that was coming.

Davis tried to rationalise, he tried to see the dog's death as one of those things that happened, but he could not. Nothing had affected him this way, and though he thought he owed it to his dead pet to feel this way, he wanted to do more. He wanted to prove his love, he wanted to spread his affection out so that everyone could see it. He wanted revenge but he didn't want it for himself; he wanted it as a woman wants a child. It was bigger than death, and smarter than genius.

The phone started to ring but he didn't answer it. He knew who it was. It was Inspector Evans. The man was brooding about the Austin deaths. The motives were too pat, the result too tidy. There was something missing; let him brood. Davis knew the Austin case was nothing. Compared to his tragedy, it was a speck on the horizon. It was nothing at all.

14

Mrs Platt couldn't bury Joey. She'd dug a grave in her garden and carried him outside, but when she looked at the hole she was overcome. She knew that she would never be able to sleep at night knowing that he was lying on his side in the cold ground, covered with dirt. No matter that he was dead, no matter that his bones were frozen and his blood was solid, and no matter that his soul was abroad, looking to reincarnate in a fresh body; in Mrs Platt's mind, Joey was still singing in his cage, his head tipped back and his eyes bright as marbles. He was still dreaming dreams he couldn't fathom, and pecking at a slice of cuttlefish. He was still fidgeting with a bell and glancing in his mirror, scratching on a sheet of sanded paper and tweeting at the unexpected twitch of a curtain.

She couldn't bury him, so she took a jam jar and popped him in that, supported by a bed of straw, his head pressed down by the lid. She put him on the sideboard, but couldn't bear to leave him with his dead eyes staring at her every time she passed, so she put him in a cupboard next to the oven. It was warm there, and if his soul didn't find a new body, it could return and settle in the corpse, knowing that it would be comfortable. Mrs Platt, satisfied she had done the right thing, made herself a cup of tea.

She liked to think about Joey, she liked to remember the days they had spent together, but she didn't like to think about the dead vet and the part she had played in his death. He had been an intense man, the sort of person who felt the depths of emotions. The sort of man who fell in love with all his heart, the sort of man Mr Platt had been. And when Mrs Platt thought about her dead husband she had to sit down, forget about a cup of tea and pour herself a gin. Guilt was the hat she wore every day, and every day gave her more guilt to wear. Joey behind the closed cupboard, the vet in a morgue fridge, Mr Platt's ashes spread beneath the garden apple tree. If she lit a candle for every ounce of guilt she felt, her rooms would burn with a brighter light than day. If guilt is a snake bite then gin is the antidote; forget the tonic but remember the lemon. If a companion's death spawns guilt, what does suicide do? Does it end the cycle of reincarnation, or does it carry the soul back to the beginning? Rats can worry themselves to death, rabbits can die of panic, elephants can die of heartache. Mrs Platt was an old lady, and she lived alone. The longer she lived the more alone she felt, and the faster she lost touch.

Bob's hat was insouciance, and he wore it with pride. Blithe as a baby in a bundle of fresh linen, he strolled into the sauna shop. Mr Henley, a man with a bad leg and bitten fingernails, got up from a desk, kick-started his feet and said, 'Help you, sir?'

'Yeah,' said Bob, smiling. 'I want to buy a sauna.'

Henley rubbed his leg in surprise. He had started his business two years before; at the time he'd been optimistic. He had done his research. The customers were there, the market was as plump as a pig and fit as a dog, the catchment area stretched from Lewes to Worthing. His bank manager was keen to lend money, so keen that he was anxious about it.

The Finns were ready to export the first batch of saunas, the showrooms were ready, the sun was shining like a smile. He had a couple of orders, and more were promised. He cleaned his teeth twice a day, and polished his shoes every morning. His suits were sharp as knives and twice as keen, and all the planets followed orbits that coalesced over his shop.

The Pines Country Club bought two of the largest models, the future unfolded in Henley's dreams like a long holiday or the poet in his heart. He bought a new car, and a mountain bike. He ate in small restaurants with long names, drank beer out of slim glasses and tried to sleep with women.

Then customers began to dry up. Recession, depression, the doldrums, a slump; whatever happened happened to Henley in a big way. Now, a week before Christmas, the bank was threatening to foreclose. And his leg had started playing up again. And he'd broken his spectacles. And lost a pair of gloves. It was all too much. He had been suicidal; it was all he could do to smile at Bob, the first potential customer in a week.

'Sauna?' said Bob, again.

'Sorry,' said Henley. 'Yes. You've come to the right place.'

Bob smiled a big one, and patted the side of the nearest cabin. 'Don't they smell nice?' he said.

Henley thought about this. 'Yes, they certainly do,' he said. 'They're electric?'

'Yes, or we can supply gas-powered models.'

'Bottled gas?'

'Yes, or mains, of course. You're particularly interested in a cabin that runs on bottled gas?'

'Not necessarily.'

'I see.'

'But I do want one I can take apart if I move…'

'No problem, sir,' said Henley. 'All these models are easily assembled…'

'And disassembled?'

'Of course.'

'Good,' said Bob, and he opened the door of one and stepped inside. He picked up a wooden ladle and rubbed its bowl.

'All the accessories are supplied free,' said Henley, 'and we throw in a couple of extra birches.'

'Do you?'

'Certainly.'

Bob stepped out of the sauna and into another.

'How big a cabin are you looking for?'

'It's just for myself.'

'Then this is the ideal one.' Henley put his hand on its roof. 'Yes.'

'You'll give me a discount for cash?'

'Cash?'

Bob patted his coat. 'That's the boy.'

'The folding stuff?'

'It's the stuff that talks.'

Henley smiled again. 'Of course,' he said.

'Then this is the one I want,' said Bob, stepping out of the cabin, 'so lead me to the dotted line.'

Henley did not stop smiling. He felt the soles of his feet begin to rise up and meet his knees, and he got a twinge in his bollocks.

'Certainly, sir,' he said.

'Bob,' said Bob.

Inspector Evans called on Sergeant Davis. He rang the bell, he knocked on the door, he crouched down and shouted through the keyhole. Then he looked through the keyhole. He could see a grey carpet, the edge of an easy chair, a brown hat, a plate of half-eaten food, the leg of a television set and a shoe. There was a pair of rolled-up socks in the shoe. The television was playing the theme from a news programme. 'Davis!' he yelled. 'Come on!' Nothing. 'Wake up! Davis!' He knocked on the door once more, then took four steps back, braced his shoulder and ran at it.

Frank spent the morning in the office. He drank three cups of tea and fiddled with a pile of Bob's colour-coded files. He ignored a couple of phone calls, and then, at midday, set out for the hospital.

He walked. The streets crunched with grit and sand, and the heaps of slush that banked the pavements were grooved with runs of water. It was a dark day, the Christmas decorations shone, and cars drove with their sidelights on. Mothers wheeled their children in pushchairs, office workers went for their lunch and old people in woolly hats shook their heads at prices; all this activity happened slowly, precisely, as if life was a dream that coursed through a lonely man's head. To Frank's eye, the edges of things were blurred, and when he tried to focus, his eyes wept at their corners.

He stopped to look in the window of a pet shop. There was an enormous tank of fish there; the strings of bubbles, fronds of weed and the darting fish captivated him, and would not let him go. He particularly liked a shoal of bright blue guppies; they swam a slow ballet, turning as one when they reached an underwater castle, disappearing behind it and emerging again higher up, where the bubbles were biggest and the light brightest. He was joined by another man; they watched together, both mesmerised by the colours and movement. No words were exchanged; Frank moved on after five minutes, and as he did he wondered if the fish saw him as he saw them. Were they amazed by his movement and his colour, by the way his clothes shimmered and his mouth opened? Did they look at their lives and think they were pointless? Frank booted a pile of grit; it exploded across the pavement, showering against the side of a car. He crossed the road and went into a florist's to buy a potted plant.

So many plants and so many flowers, so many trimmings on the floor. A friendly woman asked him what he wanted.

'Something that'll last,' he said.

'Well,' she said, picking up a flowering cactus, 'one of these'll last for ever.'

'Really?'

The woman nodded. 'It's for yourself, is it?'

Frank shook his head. 'No. It's for someone who's in hospital.'

'Oh.' The woman put the cactus down and took a step towards a shelf of less aggressive plants. 'Maybe this would be better…' She picked up something with blue flowers and glossy leaves, and handed it to him.

Frank nodded. 'Yes,' he said.

'They're always very popular.'

Frank turned it around in his hand, looked at it from every angle, nodded again and said, 'Okay. I'll take it.'

The woman smiled, but not too broadly. She could see something in Frank's eyes, something she recognised from every tragedy she had ever read. It wasn't a cloud and it wasn't a tear, it wasn't grief and it wasn't pain, but it moved between these things like a hiking devil. It cast spores into the wind and when it spoke it broke hearts; the woman was glad when Frank had paid and left the shop, but at the same time she was sad to see him go. Melancholy is a song, and though no one knows how it is written, everyone can hum the tune, and everyone can recognise the beat.

15

Inspector Evans damaged his shoulder on Sergeant Davis's door, and the injury was compounded by the fact that he failed to break it down. As he waited in out-patients, he tried to calculate how many doors he had shouldered in his life, and came up with a figure that loitered in the mid five hundreds. Then he decided to work out the accumulated poundage per square inch that his shoulder had had to put up with, but that figure eluded him. He thought about applying for compensation, but then dismissed the idea. Shouldering doors was part of the job; if he couldn't accept the risks then he was in the wrong game. He turned his thoughts to his sergeant, but when those thoughts led nowhere, he began to think about Christmas-tree lights. There was a Christmas tree in the hospital out-patients; it was decorated with ragged decorations and poorly wrapped dummy presents. A voice called his name but he didn't respond. It called again. 'Evans?' He looked up and this time he noticed. 'Me?' he said to a nurse, and she scratched her face and said, 'If your name is Evans.'

'It is,' he said.

'Come along then,' said the nurse.

Two floors above out-patients, Frank put the glossy-leaved pot-plant on a table beside Lisa's bed, and sat down. He stared at her sleeping face, listened to the steady beep of her monitor and allowed himself to be seduced. She was too vulnerable to leave, too close to forget, and the way her hair lay on the pillow broke his heart. Normally, she took such care of it, teasing it into good shape, worrying about its body and fretting about its colour; now it was lank and damp, and clotted on the linen like smoke. She was the daughter he would never have, and if she wanted, he would be the father she deserved. He would follow Bob's example and give up the agency. He would buy a shop and open a sandwich bar. He would do good in the world, and the world would smile on his cottage cheese, mayonnaise, lettuce and tomato on wholemeal. Lisa would have her baby and they could live above the shop. If she wanted, she could help with the spreading, cutting and serving, but he wouldn't put her under any obligation.

As she slept, she opened her mouth and her tongue poked out. It ran around the edges of her lips, and as it did, her eyes creased in pain. Frank got out of his chair, picked up a flannel, dipped it in a glass of water and dabbed her mouth. Her eyeballs rolled beneath their lids, she moaned a little, her head lolled and her monitor glitched. A moment later, a nurse appeared, checked the reading and forced a smile. Frank put the flannel down and said, 'How's she been?'

'No change,' she said.

'And the baby?'

The nurse shrugged. Her shoulders went up and her shoulders went down, and though she didn't say anything, Frank listened to her eyes, and they explained everything. He wished he could take them from their sockets and bowl them down narrow alleys to a week before, when everything in the world had made sense. Two weeks ago, war had had logic, and robbery had been understood. Murder and mayhem, arson and bestiality;

Frank had skirted these things, he had seen them and they'd made him cringe, but he hadn't lost sleep. Now, touched by the trouble Brighton could conjure, he rushed from intensive care, down two floors, through out-patients, past the bandaged figure of Inspector Evans, out of the hospital and into the night. He only stopped when he reached the street and had found a lamppost to lean against, and as his breath plumed into the air he kicked at a pile of snow and swore at the sky. There was a strange taste in his mouth, and his fingers tingled.

Sergeant Davis took his warrant card to the beach and tore it into tiny pieces; then he tossed it into the sky and let it fall with the snow that drifted around him. He had worked his last day as a policeman. Now he was going to murder. He was going to find a bus-driver and kill him.

Davis saw Chips in the sea and in the sky, and heard his bark in the wind that played and whistled around the girders of the pier. He felt the dog's hair in the air and remembered the longing in the dog's eyes; revenge was going to become the man's life, and would fill his days. He had not made many important decisions in his life, but this was the big one. It barked and it growled, and it grew to the size of a wolf-hound. It nuzzled his face and slobbered in his ear. 'Okay,' said the ex-policeman, and then he left the beach and walked back into town.

No one met Mrs Austin; she stood on Brighton station for ten minutes, then dragged her suitcase to the taxi-rank, and asked to be taken to a decent hotel.

'What you mean, decent?' said the driver.

'Clean,' said Mrs Austin. 'Hot and cold in all rooms.'

'Okay.'

She sat back for the drive, and as she stared at the busy streets, the panic and pain the news had provoked was displaced by regret. God's will was overwhelming, but she could not stop herself thinking that she should have been with her children, that she could have prevented the tragedy. It should never have happened. It doesn't matter how old your children are, they will always be your children, and carry an echo of your nursing arms. She mumbled incoherently; the driver looked at her in his mirror, and shrugged. She put the tips of her fingers together and closed her eyes... The eye of the Lord is upon them that fear him, upon him that hope in his mercy; to deliver their soul from death, and to keep them alive in famine...

'This'll do you,' said the driver. He had stopped outside the Atlas Hotel.

Mrs Austin blinked and looked up at it. 'Yes,' she said softly. 'It looks fine.' She smiled, and reached for her handbag. 'Thank you.'

Mrs Platt had learnt that revenge compounds tragedy, it cannot relieve it. Now, as her kitchen clock crept towards midnight, she set the jam-jarred Joey in the middle of the table and lit four candles. She was going to contact the spirits of her dead bird and the dead vet, and she was going to ask for forgiveness. She was going to ask them how she could redeem herself. She was willing to do anything to assuage the guilt she felt. Her mind was full and her body craved some nostrum; she sat down and laid her hands palms down on the table, closed her eyes and began to whisper a solemn invocation. These were words that could be destroyed by copying, rendered useless by writing, words that had been passed from mother to daughter and from daughter to child. 'Spirits of the night, protectors of the spirits and ghosts of all sentient beings, remind me, be with me and give me the keys to your orbit. I am here and you are there, and our realms meet at this table.' She took a deep breath, opened her eyes a tad, drummed her fingers and waited.

Joey sat in his jar, and his fading feathers teemed with a million microscopic mites. The candles guttered and a breeze rattled the kitchen window; Mrs Platt closed her eyes, and began to whisper again.

'Spirits of the night, protectors of the spirits and ghosts of all sentient beings, remind me, be with me and give me the keys to your orbit. Clatter your keys and display yourselves. Show me the strength of your purpose, and explain yourselves. Give me a taste of your power, justify yourselves and let me hear your voices.' Her voice wavered, a ball of phlegm popped in her throat and the candles guttered again, but this time no breeze could be felt in the room. Now, the atmosphere was warm and heavy, and scented with roses. Roses in borders and roses on graves, roses in bouquets and roses in a virgin's hair; the spirits smell of roses, and as they began to gather around Mrs Platt, they smelt themselves, and they smelt her. They prided themselves on their compassion, and when they looked at the woman, her bird in a jar and the four candles, and when they heard the incantation, they began to take form in the air above her, and to suspend time.

Bob's sauna almost filled his living-room; as he waited for it to reach optimum temperature, he smiled and congratulated himself. The showroom had distorted its size, but as he undressed, he didn't care. He wanted the deep cleaning experience, and a skin of open pores bleeding the taste of the last meal he'd eaten. A big box of heat; it was fitted with a light that went off when it was ready for use. Bob was a patient man; he lay naked on his sofa and traced patterns on his chest.

Mrs Austin booked into the Atlas. She sat on her bed, stared at the wallpaper, and then phoned the police. A desk sergeant tried to connnect her with Evans, but the man had gone off duty. 'Then you'll take a message,' said Mrs Austin.
   'Madam?'
   'I'm Cyril and Diana Austin's mother.'
   'Austin?'
   'Yes.'
   'The murder?'
   Mrs Austin's throat cramped, then relaxed, then cramped again, then relaxed again. 'The inspector phoned me in Canter-bury; I was asked to come down to —' she took a deep breath

'to identify their bodies. I'm staying at the Atlas. Would you ask him to phone me in the morning.'

'The Atlas.'

'Yes.'

'Mrs Austin?'

'Correct.'

The desk sergeant's pen ran out. He looked at it, shook it, breathed on it, then tossed it into a wastepaper-basket. He picked up another and scribbled on the corner of a sheet of paper. 'The Atlas...' he repeated. 'Number?'

Mrs Austin boiled. 'Don't you have a telephone directory?' she snapped, and she put the phone down. She stood up and walked to the window. She looked down at the street, and watched a slow fall of snow drift across the sky. When Cyril was a boy, snow had been his delight, and his sister had helped him build snowmen in the garden. That old garden in Canterbury, with the shade of apple and pear trees, and old shrubberies. She felt in her pocket and pulled out the handkerchief the man on the train had given her. She put it to her nose and blew hard. 'Children,' she whispered at the window, and it rattled back, from the joy of another town to the numbing of Brighton.

Mrs Platt felt the spirits as they gathered above her, but she did not open her eyes. She focused on the backs of her eyelids and repeated her incantation. She saw spots of light and sheets of dark against the spots; she kept her hands on the table and took deep, steady breaths. The spirits concentrated their strength, they directed their power at Joey's jam jar and then they began to move it.

It began by moving slowly and steadily from side to side, rucking the table-cloth as it did, and a low whistle came from its lid. As soon as Mrs Platt heard this, she opened her eyes and her body filled with heat. The spirits descended and surrounded her, swirling like water around a stranded rock. The jam jar was shivering, the whistling raised its pitch, the crockery on the kitchen shelves began to rattle, and an egg-cup fell and smashed on the floor. The smell of roses rose and fell like a ship at sea, and began to clog her nostrils. One spirit touched her skin, and then another, and then another, and then they were forcing themselves beneath her clothes, rubbing her stomach and pinching the loose skin on her arms. One nestled in her armpits, and others found homes in the creases of her stomach. When they came into contact with her skin they began to multiply, and they encouraged each other by whispering and singing. Their phantom lips tickled Mrs Platt, but she didn't mind. She didn't mind at all, she didn't want them to leave her. She was reminded of Mr Platt, and she remembered long summer days, plump fruit and long grass. A sweet and musical brook, the smell of his hair and his fingers' touch. She felt his revenant fold its arms around her waist, and it murmured in her ear. She could see his eyes and they watched her, and she said his name. The word smashed the air, and it shattered the mood; the spirits released their grip, and began to dissolve. They were not afraid but they were unsettled; they gathered together by the window, and they looked out at the night. Snow washed the sky, covered the garden and weighed the branches of an old apple tree; Mrs Platt said her husband's name again and the spirits popped, and then disappeared. She felt refreshed, as if she'd just stepped out of the bath. She ran her hands through her hair and felt like a girl getting ready for an exciting date. She looked at Joey in the jar. His feathers were bright and shiny. She believed in other worlds, in the mysteries of reincarnation and the riddles in a spirit's gift. She smelt roses and she felt warm. 'Fred,' she said, and then she stood up and went to make a cup of tea.

16

Davis walked through the night, and his spirit was swathed and then overtaken by darkness. It came up on his blindside, tapped one shoulder and then the other, and it laughed its persuasion. If Chips could have spoken to him, he would have told him to stop. Revenge was not worth dignifying with pain. Life goes on. Buy another dog, change your job, move to another town. Do anything but choose a bus-driver at random, ask him an innocent question and kill him. Do anything but compound the grief, do anything but allow yourself this luxury. Go for a long walk, write a poem, learn to speak Italian. Book a holiday in Lapland, start collecting postcards of stained-glass windows, learn Irish history. Find out all you can about the dynamics of amateur psychology. Bleed knowledge and laugh at people who smoke. How many things can fill a man's head?

Davis walked from the front to the bus station, along the streets of closed shops, under the strings of decorations that swung and illuminated the night. When he passed the entrance to a pub, a pair of drunks forced him to step off the pavement and walk through a pile of slush. One stared at him, and said, 'What you doing, shit-head?'

The second drunk laughed, focused and spat.

'Yeah, shit-head,' said the first.

Davis looked over his shoulder at the two men. The second was bent double, holding his stomach; the first had a large head and short hair. 'I'm sorry?' said Davis.

'Shit-head,' said the drunk, and he took two aggressive steps towards Davis.

'You're talking to me?' said Davis.

'Bet your arse.'

Now Davis took two steps towards the drunk, narrowed his eyes and balled his fingers. He began to seep the scent that animals weep before they set themselves for a fight, and the drunk sensed it. He drew himself up and said, 'Going to do something about it?'

'Do?' said Davis. 'Do?'

'Yeah.'

'Do?'

'You heard me.'

Now Davis laughed, and the laugh came from deep in his stomach, from a dangerous and willing spot. He looked at the other drunk. The other drunk was puking, shooting a slim river of bile on to the pavement and clutching himself around the waist. A faint curtain of snow was falling, settling on the men's hair and coats. 'Yeah,' said Davis, 'I think I am going to do something about it.'

And the able drunk laughed.

'Anyone ever tell you that you're an ugly bastard?' said Davis.

The drunk's mouth dropped open, and he fixed his feet solid to the pavement. He let the words fidget in his head, and they spelt themselves for him. 'What?' he said.

'You heard,' said Davis, and then he hit the drunk a quick one in the stomach. He had a hard punch, a snappy thing all fist and physics, and as the man doubled, he sliced him across the back of the neck. 'No one calls me that.'

The other drunk looked up from his sick, saw his friend writhing, saw Davis standing and watching, and he puked again.

'No one,' said Davis.

The first drunk pulled himself to his knees and wiped some blood from his mouth, but Davis kicked him down again. A woman came from the pub and saw the scene. She ran back inside and screamed for help, but before she reappeared, Davis was away up the street, turning a corner and whistling 'Invitation to the Blues', an old song.

It was a mile to the bus station, but he didn't hurry. On the corner of Break Street and South Road, he stopped to watch a woman walk her dog. This was a mongrel, a hairy black and white terrier/collie cross, an intelligent-looking animal with a big waggy tail and flat feet. It stopped to shit by a lamppost; the woman looked the other way as it dropped the turd, then said, 'Well done, Bruce.'

'Bruce?' said Davis, softly. He believed in dog names for dogs, but he didn't have a thing about it. Not a thing like he had about bus-drivers. They had no defence. They could think but they didn't think clearly or enough. He saw that now, and understood his reason for living.

Bob sat in his sauna and sweltered. Sweat streamed from his forehead, over his cheeks, down his neck and on to his chest. He ladled some water on to the rocks, the steam hissed and rose; he leant back and closed his eyes.

He felt his life was just beginning, and he began to feel released. He was light and seemed to float above the world. The heat manumitted his heart, and set it off down a bright and comfortable road. How many obligations had once followed him, and how many times had he felt that other people were controlling him? From his father to his teachers, to his first boss and to his bank manager. His wife. His children. Frank. His building society, the shoes he walked in and the sky above. Everyone has a release and Bob had found his. He smiled at his good fortune, but he wasn't smug about it. He had worked hard, he had accumulated debt but he didn't lose sleep over it. Money meant nothing to him.

The sauna was lit by a dim bulb, enough to see the shape of a hand in front of a face, and enough to see the door handle glint, but that was all. The fresh yellow of the wooden seat was its own shadow, and the steam that rose all around thickened. Bob's pores began to relax and give themselves all the time they needed. He stood up, spread a towel on the floor, tossed another splash at the rocks and then lay down. He stared at the ceiling, counted to twenty and then closed his eyes.

He slipped into that drifty place that whistles between awake and asleep, and his thoughts settled on memories of his sister, Deborah. Never Debbie, never, ever; born with palsy, she could do nothing for herself, but she could see different and perfect worlds teeming over the backs of her hands. She spent her entire life in a wheelchair, dribbled a lot, and sung with an atonal voice that forced tears from marble. Bob had understood Deborah and she had understood him; he had felt her frustration and had understood her triumphs. No one else came close. She had triumphed when she nodded her head in time with 'Kentucky Avenue'. Deborah with the unfocused eyes, the yellow finger-nails and the tiny feet. Dead now, stolen at sixteen and buried in a plot only Bob visits. Dead girl in the ground, dead girl with curls on her head she could never brush. Crease, gods; kill some rattlesnakes with a trowel or prove that you care. Bob always wore a suit to the cemetery, and carried flowers to the grave.

Frank sat beside Lisa and held her hand. She was living in a slice of the world that most people never see, a place where the senses are heightened by pain and given new toys to play with. She felt his grip on her hand, and she smelt him, and though she wanted to open her eyes, she couldn't. She could feel her baby as it raged against the walls of her womb, and it filled her mouth with the taste of liquorice. Her head filled with a jumble of memories that rearranged themselves in bizarre stacks. One minute she was back in the chemist's shop, standing on a ladder to tidy a shelf of perfume, but the perfume wasn't in bottles, it was in porcelain envelopes. Then she was in her flat, and Frank came down to talk to her. He rode a motor bike around her kitchenette, filling the place with exhaust fumes. He was choking her. She spasmed and coughed. She opened her mouth and tried to say something, but the words stuck in her head. She tried to rub her chest but her arms were tied. Her three machines beeped, tweeked and dripped. Frank stood up and called for a nurse. 'Nurse?'

'Yes?' said the nurse. She strolled into the room, adjusted her dress, licked some cake crumbs from her fingers and glanced at the monitors.

'I think she was trying to tell me something.' Frank's voice was cracking at the edges, and flakes of it were lying on the floor.

The nurse tapped a screen with her finger, tweeked a knob and shook her head. 'She's okay,' she said.

'That's debatable,' said Frank.

The nurse gave him a look only a nurse can give, a meld of arrogance, compassion, impatience and sex. With her red hair and her flat forehead, her fat thighs and her big hands, she made Frank angry. A little power in the hands of a nobody is a dangerous thing; it absorbs a dead personality and magnifies itself, and sticks in the eyes. 'Debatable?' said the nurse. 'And you know something I don't?'

'What?' There was something about her voice, something that reminded Frank.

'About this condition.' She looked at Lisa and crossed her arms.

Frank said, 'No.' It was in the centre of her voice, a deceit she could not conceal.

'Then what are you trying to say?'

'Did you train?'

'I beg your pardon?'

'Did you train to be like this?' Frank knew now; the nurse had Janet Black's voice, winging its way across thirty years and landing with a slap on his forehead.

'I'm an SRN.'

'Is that all?' said Frank. Janet Black and the pain of those beautiful boots. Spanish hand-tooled leather; they clacked on pavements like a come-on. He licked his lips, he filled with a thousand pains and memories. He had failed and the failure cut. His life was reducing itself, tumbling through regret and chaos, death and insult. Something Bob had said, something about the futility of the agency's work, came to him, and he found himself agreeing. The importance of life was grown from grief, longing, hope and wounds.

The nurse narrowed her eyes, and said, 'I think you'd better leave now.'

'You think?' said Frank. 'My God.' He stood up and rubbed the back of Lisa's hand while his words sank into the nurse's head. He had loved Janet Black, but one warm day she had told him that he made her cringe. 'That's extraordinary.' Neither of them noticed, but Lisa opened one of her eyes and smiled at the ceiling; her pain had dulled for a moment, and all her troubles were reduced to nothing. She tried to turn her head but the thought brought the pain back with a crack. Her machines watched her and Frank left. The nurse worked on what he had said but couldn't get past the idea that he was making fun of her. But how? How and why? She shrugged and went back to the staff room.

Davis reached the bus station at half-past ten. The place was quiet; a few drunks were loitering around the toilets, and an inspector was writing in his notebook. A cat appeared and rubbed itself against Davis's leg; he reached down and stroked it, and made purring sounds through his teeth, then bought a cup of coffee from a van and settled down on a bench to drink it.

He waited for ten minutes before a late bus pulled up, dropped a raggle of passengers, and reversed into the garage. The driver sat in his seat to complete his log, then opened the door, jumped down and strolled to a rest-room. Davis finished his coffee, said goodbye to the cat and meandered across the pull-ins, and leant against a photo-booth. He was wearing a leather jacket; he zipped it to his neck. He was wearing a baseball hat; he pulled it over his eyes and steadied his breathing. It plumed in the freezing air. The moon slipped behind a slash of cloud, and a few flakes of snow drifted out of the sky and settled on his head. It was a still and perfect winter night, as sharp as a knife. Two minutes later, the driver came from the rest-room, called 'Goodnight!' to someone, patted the side of his bus and left the garage.

He passed twenty feet in front of Davis. He was a young man with a round, baby face, a loping walk and long brown hair tied in a pony-tail. Davis loathed babies and pony-tails. He waited a minute, then followed.

He was careful and walked with deliberate, steady steps. He waited when the driver stopped to look at televisions in a shop window, and ducked into a doorway when the man suddenly turned and started to walk back the way he'd come. Then, for no reason at all, he turned again and carried on, crossing the road in a long diagonal; he checked his pockets for change, then went into the Lamb and Flag.

Davis didn't like pubs; he hated the smoke, the music and the lights, and he hated the false smiles and greetings of barmen, and he hated the effect alcohol had on people. People should keep their bodies pure. They shouldn't allow poisons to alter the way they behaved. They should keep their fingernails clean and they shouldn't have to listen to pop music if they didn't want to. And most of all he hated pubs because of something that had happened when Chips was alive. He'd gone to a pub with the dog and been ordered to leave immediately. What had been the problem? It was a blameless animal, free of guilt and poison. It had stared up at the bar with trust in its eyes, and its reward had been the door.

But revenge knows no restrictions, no barriers, frontiers and no dreamland; it is a pure thing, like a baby's thoughts. It's a slice of life that's missing worry; Davis followed the driver into the Lamb and Flag, ordered a tonic water and sat down. He scanned the faces for his man, but couldn't see him; then he saw him come from the toilets, kiss a woman and sit down six feet away.

This woman was blonde, wore glasses and had a small, pinched mouth. Davis was scared of women, frightened of their hips and lips and alarmed by their voices. Some WPCs had reduced him to nausea and half a day off; the scent of their perfume or a sight of their hairless legs or the smell of their locker room or their talk. Their talk about anything. He had never made love, he had never sat in a chair with a woman in a chair opposite and wished himself into her arms, and he'd never stumbled over words he'd said but wished he hadn't. He'd never said something like 'Would you like to stay over?' and then felt the words slamming back at him later, battering him with longing and guilt. He'd never laid awake all night and wished that a woman would write or phone or think about him, a woman with light curly hair and a voice like a song you've heard but can't quite remember. He'd never shared a lift with a woman whose scent overwhelmed him, a scent of trees, sex and another man, and he'd never prayed that a woman who wore cycling shorts would send him a record by Little Anthony and the Imperials because it reminded her of him. He'd never planned a holiday in St Albans or Kent with a woman who clung to his waist and said, 'Yeah, I fancy it like mad.' He'd never nodded with drink and salted nuts and watched a woman slip out of a beige two-piece suit, expensive underwear and soft leather shoes. He'd never smoked dope in bed, made love, smoked some more and then made love again. He'd never slipped into a shower and made it like a rabbit and not known what he was doing until the water turned cold, and she'd yelled and bit his neck. He drank tonic water because it was strong. He'd never made love while an old film had been shown on the television, and he'd never scratched a woman's name on his skin. He'd never been to Paris for five days and missed all the sights. He'd never had a woman offer to cover herself with carbonara sauce and do him in Italian. He'd never laid naked on the deck of a Greek fishing boat, and dreamt himself in love. He'd never sat in a club with a woman he never imagined would look at him twice, and found that she was staring at him with big eyes, glistening lips and an unbuttoned blouse. He had never unbuttoned a blouse. No woman had ever slipped her arms around his waist and whispered, 'You've burnt your name in me.' No woman had made plans and then changed them because he had walked across a room and said, 'Good evening.' He'd never heard a saxophone and willed himself into the head of the man who was playing, and he'd never eaten a meal he didn't like because it was the route to a woman's mouth. A woman had never sat up all night and realised that she had ruined her life for him, and no one had ever bought him a present that cost £355. He'd never sat in a field and been told that he looked like some film star, or some pop star, or some old star, or some star anyway. Any star, anywhere. Who cares? Davis didn't. He leaned back, sipped his drink and watched his bus-driver, and

wished him a happy evening with the blonde. He would sit for
as long as it took, then follow the man home. He would note
his address and he would take his time. He would go home
and dream a sweet and blameless sleep, and he would wake
with a fresh head. He would eat his breakfast and think about
Chips, and remember how the dog had sat up on his hind legs
for a cornflake. Davis lived in a world that nudged reality but
refused to talk to it. He was in control, more control than he
had ever imagined.

Mrs Platt dreamed a sweet and blameless sleep, and it was
watched over by a legion of kind spirits. They swilled and
tangoed around her head, and they murmured their comfort
to her. They offered to carry her away with them, to cradle her
in their invisible arms and soothe her troubles. She nodded and
smiled in her sleep, and whispered her assent. Her heart slowed
and her blood slackened in her veins. Her memories met her
pain and calmed it, her thoughts tumbled and fell to nothing.
The spirits stroked her forehead and touched the tips of her
fingers; she turned over, and tried to open her eyes, but they
wouldn't move. She wasn't troubled, she felt less trouble than
she had ever felt, she felt free and sweet. There was music in
her room, bells and strings, and the soft tap of a foot. A spirit
whispered, 'You are mine,' and another whistled a medley of
songs from the 1920s. It was half-past five in the morning, the
snow lay on the roof of her house and covered the branches
of her garden trees. Mrs Platt did not stop smiling, and she
was not afraid.

17

At half-past seven in the morning, the thief visited Lisa, and
her embryo gave up and slipped from her body. She felt the
miscarriage as an echo against the wall of her womb, a hot
and stabbing thud, and then her body began to collapse from

the inside out. She yelled for a nurse, and one came running. 'I've lost it!' she wailed.

'Have you?' said the nurse.

Lisa nodded.

The nurse smiled indulgently, adjusted her glasses, clicked a pen and put it in her pocket. 'We'll see about that,' she said, as if she could do something about it, and she began to peel the bedclothes back.

Lisa grabbed them and held them to her chin, and hissed, 'What's the matter with you? Why don't you believe me? Why do you have to treat me like an idiot, like I don't know what's happening to my own body?' She took a breath. 'You take a couple of exams, get to wear a uniform and you think you're God.' She put a hand between her legs, dabbed at the mess and held it up. Mucus, blood and fluids ran down her fingers, slid across her wrist and dripped on to the sheets. 'I think I know what I'm talking about, don't you?'

Now the nurse paled, nodded and ran for help. It came a minute later; one doctor and two more nurses, flapping down the corridor and through the ward door, wiping biscuit crumbs from their mouths and adjusting their glasses. Lisa had collapsed back on to the bed, and her face was streaked with blood. She opened her eyes and saw the blurred outlines of faces, and then they were gone, the baby was gone, Frank wasn't there, the pain was sliding in and around her, she felt as though all the fluid in her body had been sucked out and frozen into a block. She put her arms out and thought she felt it on the bed beside her. It burnt her fingers and blistered their tips; she opened her mouth to scream, but no sound came out. Her breath dropped on to the bed and nestled against her body; then it was lost as she felt her body being lifted up and laid on fresh sheets. She heard the sound of metal on metal, a syringe filled and a sudden rush of beeps from a monitor. Adrian's face floated by, then her father's, then some face she didn't recognise. It had big teeth and pale cheeks; it leaned towards her and said something. Then she felt the needle, a quick rush and then silence, a big quiet that came wrapped in warmth and covered her completely.

Inspector Evans waited in vain. He scratched his head. He had tried to phone his sergeant but his sergeant wasn't answering the phone. He rubbed his shoulder and went to see the Superintendent.

The Super was standing in his office, watching the snow, drinking a cup of tea and thinking about golf. He was a quiet man, and shared his inspector's concerns. 'Give him another day; if he hasn't called in, go round and see him.'

'It's not like Davis.'

'No,' said the Super, and he moved to his desk and sat down. 'But there's a lot of flu around. I expect he's gone to bed, taken the phone off the hook and decided to ignore the door.'

Evans nodded, but he wasn't convinced. He was going to say something else about Davis, something about recent behaviour, but the Super changed the subject.

'What's the score on the Austin case?'

Evans shook his head. 'Three nil.'

'Any chance of a score draw?'

'We're going nowhere. No witnesses. Any motives were lost before we had a chance to speak to the victims, and the only people who might have had an idea turn out to have no idea at all.'

'And they are?'

'A couple of privates Mr Austin hired to follow his wife.'

'They're not in the frame?'

'No.'

'Sure about that?'

Evans thought about Frank and Bob, he pictured their faces, and then nodded. 'They're not even close to it.'

'I see.'

'We've got the mother down to identify the bodies, but I don't think she's going to shed any light.'

'Why not?'

Evans shrugged. 'Why should she?'

'You've met her?'

'Later.'

'Mmm…' The Super put the tips of his fingers together and pressed them together until the whites of the knuckles showed. He leaned back, stared at the ceiling and imagined a perfect approach shot to the eighteenth green at Wentworth, a full house rising to him, the sun shining, a six-foot putt remaining for victory.

Evans coughed and waited. He thought about Frank and Bob again, then stopped.

The Super crouched and lined up the shot.

Evans stood up.

It was only six feet, but the green had an awkward camber. This was pressure golf, but he had been born for this moment, and was not going to let himself down. You get one life and if you don't live it the way you want, then you've only got yourself to blame. Discover your own faults and you discover yourself — cure the faults in your swing, your approach play, your putting — golf is life. You get one ball and one course, and the most satisfying courses are the most difficult ones. He tapped the green with his putter, and concentrated.

Evans recognised the look in his boss's eyes. He wished he was at home with Mrs Evans, fixing the Christmas-tree lights and helping to hang paper chains across the living-room. The ones you buy in a newsagent's and make yourself by gluing coloured strips of paper together. He turned and went to the door.

The Super felt his arms go rigid; he did some deep breathing, then presented his club-face to the ball.

Evans put his hand on the doorknob.

The spectators hushed.

Evans turned the knob and opened the door. It was stiff, and squeaked on its hinge.

The Super drew back his putter and hit the ball. It began to roll towards the hole.

Evans stepped into the corridor as the ball dropped into the hole and two thousand people stood and cheered. The Super looked down from the ceiling, called, 'Do your best,' to Evans, and then buzzed for his secretary.

Davis woke with a fresh head. As he ate his breakfast, he missed Chips so much that he started to talk as if the dog was there. 'What shall we do today?' he said. 'Go for a walk or watch some telly?' He looked at the floor, imagined an answer and said, 'Okay.' He carried his bowl of cornflakes to his sitting-room, switched on the television and sat down.

A smooth man was talking to a roomful of people about legalising drugs. 'So the Dutch experiment appears to have some merits…'

'I'd disagree.'

'That's to be expected.'

'As is that.'

'Let's try and keep this discussion on an even keel.'

'Control the supply and you control the use…'

'Control the supply and you criminalise the state…'

'The state's the biggest criminal of all!'

'Decriminalisation is the first step…'

Davis hopped to another channel. A thin woman with red hair and a lopsided smile was talking about how the key to body fitness was 'little and often'. Then she stood up, stepped into a cleared space and demonstrated a series of exercises that involved stretching and twisting from the waist. She was wearing a tight leotard; Davis blanched, hopped again and found a schools' programme about dam building in Brazil. A tribe of natives and thousands of unique species were threatened by the construction, but the hydroelectric power that the dam would generate was needed if Brazil was going to modernise its industry and infrastructure. A politician explained that sacrifices had to be made; his arguments were contradicted by an environmentalist, who stood on a hill overlooking a devasted rain forest and waved his arms. He wished that his arms were wings and that he could fly away, but he couldn't so he stayed and fought against the chaos in his country. He had survived an attempt on his life, and vilification in the press, but he laughed at the politician. He was a brave man, and wore shorts. The politician had small, green eyes and his hair was too big for his age. 'Brazil,' he said, 'is meeting the challenge of the twenty-first century with courage and vigour.' The environmentalist shook his head and said, 'Brazil is heading for disaster. Unless we listen to our hearts, we will not even reach the twenty-first century. The thief is at the gate, and it has stolen the key.' Then the programme switched to a studio, and a small man with a beard and an easy smile who said, 'So, there we have it. First of all, we must decide if we're going to take sides, or are both these men making valid points?' 'Fuck knows,' said Davis, and he hopped to the next channel and a round-up of the previous day's financial news.

A mobile-phone company had gone under; the company had either been 'very stupid, or made a brave attempt to break into a very competitive market. And now, let's take a look at the markets.'

'Let's not,' said Davis, and he flicked the television off, finished his cornflakes, and said, 'Come on,' to the floor, 'let's go for a walk.'

Evans met Mrs Austin at the Atlas and drove her to the mortuary. He attempted small talk, but she was frank and direct. 'What happened,' she said, 'exactly?'

'You haven't been told?'

'No.'

'Well...' Evans had told hundreds of people the worst news, but the job never got easier. Every time he had to do it, he felt his throat freeze and his ears began to sing.

'Please.' Mrs Austin reassured him. 'I lost my husband in a car accident, my sister was killed in the war.' Her voice was flat. 'I can take it.'

'Mrs Austin, your daughter-in-law...'

'Sandie…'

'Yes. She was found with her throat cut; our first thought was to interview your son, but before we got to him he was found floating off the Palace Pier. He'd drowned.'

'Drowned?'

'I'm sorry.'

Mrs Austin shook her head. Evans stopped at traffic lights and looked at her. Her hands were lying in her lap, she stared ahead, she didn't blink. 'You think Cyril murdered Sandie?'

'No,' said Evans. 'I didn't say that.'

'But you wanted to interview him.'

'We wanted to interview anyone connected with your daughter-in-law.'

'So you spoke to Diana, before…'

'No.' The lights changed. 'She was dead before we met.' Evans looked at Mrs Austin. 'She…' he said, as a car honked behind him. He dropped into gear and moved off.

'She?'

'She threw herself off Beachy Head.'

Now Mrs Austin rummaged for a handkerchief. She balled it in her fist; they turned left, then right, then right again. When they reached the mortuary, they sat and stared at a sign that read 'Official vehicles only', and the atmosphere in the car drifted between pain and fear. Evans said, 'I'm sorry.' The words slid down his chin and smeared the front of his shirt. He felt disgusted with himself, angry with everything and humbled by Mrs Austin. She looked calm, absolutely in control.

She felt numb and very old, though a lively guilt was biting her gut, nibbling its edges and folding the corners. 'I should have been with them,' she said.

'What good would that have done?'

Mrs Austin didn't answer. She stared ahead and then she climbed out of the car and walked to the mortuary.

Frank sat on Lisa's bed and held her hand. She smelt of almonds and antiseptic, and her face looked as though it were snowing.

A phone was ringing in another part of the hospital, and feet clattered down the corridors, but Frank heard nothing. He saw something in the shape of her mouth and the scatter of her hair on the pillow, the hint of a wish he'd had years before. Janet Black and a flat on the top floor of an old house, a view of the sea, long Friday nights in a comfortable pub, Saturday-afternoon walks on the Downs, Sunday morning in bed. Boots that didn't pinch. A baby in his arms, and now, Frank thought, I hold my baby's hand. He said a prayer to the bed, slow words he pulled from some forgotten loft in his head.

A nurse he hadn't seen before came and tapped Lisa's monitor, looked at a chart, checked her watch and ticked the chart. She looked at Frank and said, 'Still here?'

'I love her,' he said. He felt a hole in his heart, and put a hand to his chest. 'She's all I've got.'

'She's going to be fine,' said the nurse, and she gave an encouraging smile that leapt into Frank's eyes, sat down and did not betray itself.

'Is she?' he said. 'Really?'

'Yes.'

Frank let out a deep sigh.

'All the signs are good. She's lost a lot of blood, and of course the miscarriage gave her body a shock, but she's strong. Don't worry,' she said, and she put her hand on Frank's shoulder. 'Be positive, that's the best thing you can do for her.' She smiled again. 'You're the best dad she could have.'

Frank opened his mouth, but then he stopped himself. He turned back to Lisa and stroked the back of her hand. All his wishes gathered in his mind and smiled at him. 'Thanks,' he said.

'You're welcome.'

Davis stood opposite his chosen bus-driver's house, and leant against a lamppost. The day had changed the place. The night before, when he had stood at the same spot and watched the driver let himself in, the house had looked smaller, and had

123

matched his mood. Now the domesticity of the scene bothered him. There was a bird-table in the man's front garden,
a bicycle by the front door and Christmas lights in the front-
room window. A pint of milk was standing on the doorstep,
and snowy footprints were scattered up and down the path.
How easy was it to kill a man? Did it become more difficult
as you learnt more about your victim, or easier? When he
was face to face with the driver, and when he held a knife to
the man's throat, would saying 'Goodbye' help expunge the
guilt? A man with a dog walked by and nodded 'Hello'; Davis grunted and shaded his face beneath the brim of his hat.
When he looked up again, the milk bottle had been removed
from the step, and a curtain twitched in an upstairs window.
He imagined; the blonde he had seen in the pub rubbing the
sleep from her eyes, staring at the winter and then walking
to the bathroom. The driver padding about in his dressing-
gown, scratching his head, holding up his pyjama trousers
with one hand. A warm and comfortable kitchen, a pot of
tea on the table, toast browning under the grill, a shelf of
healthy pot-plants, condensation running down the glass. A
fresh newspaper. A radio warbling in the background, and
the smell of hot water and soap drifting downstairs. Did the
driver have a pet? Maybe a dog was waiting for a cornflake, or
a cat was prowling for a bowl of milk, rubbing itself against
a leg or the side of a kitchen cabinet. Or there was a goldfish
called Henry, and it lived in a bowl by the microwave. The
driver pursed his lips at it and crumbled some food into its
water; the perfect animal for the age, with rubber weed, a
rubber castle and coloured glass. Davis was jealous, and this
jealousy hardened his resolve. Some people had all the luck,
some people didn't appreciate their lives. And when he remembered Chips, and all the things they had done together,
this resolve solidified. The equation was immutable. Guilt
did not affect it. All Davis's instincts were buried in the pain
of his loss, and the loss of sense. He walked fifty yards down
the street, and went into a café for a cup of coffee. He sat at

the window and drank slowly, and he watched the driver's front gate with dull, flat eyes.

Bob glowed. He shone. His eyes gleamed. His head was polished and his chest was burnished. When he spoke, the words came out sleeked, like tropical leaves. His lips were big and rubbery, and his teeth were polished. He felt as good as he had ever done. He had owned a sauna for twenty-four hours, and had spent sixteen of them in it. He had only slept for four, but felt as though he'd had ten, and he didn't feel hungry. He slapped his stomach, slipped into a clean shirt and a pair of beige slacks, and went to see Frank.

He found him in the office, tipped back in his chair with his legs on the desk. He was listening to the radio, and said, 'You'll like this.'

'What?' said Bob.

'I just heard it. When they first tried to sell Coca-Cola in China, they discovered that it sounds like "Bite the wax tadpole" in Cantonese.'

'What does?'

'Coca-Cola.'

'What? The drink or the name?'

'The name, Bob.'

'Fascinating.'

'I knew you'd think so.'

'I do,' said Bob, and he sat down.

The office was cold and beginning to acquire the patina of disuse; there was a musty smell in the place, and dust on the telephone.

'Busy?' said Bob.

'Who?' said Frank. 'Me?'

'If you like.'

Frank stared at his old friend, and decided that he'd never seen him look healthier. This reinforced the feeling, the creeping idea that the man had been right all along. The agency was a waste of time. The work was a deceit, it bred its own chaos.

This wasn't a life, this wasn't where he should be. He should have stayed with Lisa. 'No,' he said. 'The phone's rung a couple of times, but I couldn't be bothered.'

'What does this mean?'

Frank shrugged.

'Can I assume you've decided not to have the agency?'

'Oh yes,' said Frank. 'You can do that.'

'Good.'

'It's all yours.'

Bob laughed. 'I don't think so...'

Frank laughed. The sound shocked him, and gave him a pain in the chest.

'...I'll put it on the market.'

Frank took his feet off the desk and a hand over his heart. 'I think I'm beginning to feel like you.'

'Healthy?'

'No...'

'Pissed?'

'Pissed off.' Frank rubbed his forehead. 'I think I'm going to follow you. We're in a stupid game.'

'Hey,' said Bob, 'I'm out of it.'

'You always were too clever for your own good.' He smiled, weakly. 'Does it feel good?'

'Better than good.' Bob stretched his arms above his head and took a deep breath. 'I bought a sauna. You've got to come round and have one; once you've got those pores open, you'll think you're a different person.'

'Sounds like what I need.'

'Believe me.'

Frank looked at his friend and he did. He didn't need to think about it, and he didn't need to say anything else.

As the evening lowered over Brighton, Lisa slept, Evans drove home and got caught in a traffic jam. Erica Austin sat in her hotel bedroom, and spread her children's effects on the bed. A wedding ring, a pair of watches, a purse and a wallet. She had been told that she could return to Canterbury whenever she wanted, but she didn't want, she didn't want at all.

And as the evening thickened. Bob fired up his sauna, Davis sat on his bus-driver's bus and watched the back of the man's head, and Frank let himself into Mrs Platt's house. He climbed the stairs, waited on the third for a moment, then walked back down and banged on his landlady's door. When there was no reply, he bent down and looked through the keyhole. He saw nothing. He smelt nothing and he heard nothing, but he felt something. This was a musty thing that seeped from the the the hole and the cracks around the door, and it shivered into his eye, rattled around his head and dived into his spine. He stood up and banged again, waited another moment, put his hand on the doorknob and turned it. The door creaked open, and the musty feeling gathered around Frank, and pulled him into the room. 'Mrs Platt?' he said. 'Hello?' His words echoed off the furniture and settled against the walls. The air was freezing and burnt the back of his throat. An old photograph of a starched Victorian family glared down at him, and a pile of ashes filled the cold grate. Joey's empty cage stood in one corner, the water bowl full of dusty water, and a maize stick propped against the bars. A pair of wineglasses and some dead candles stood on a sideboard, and the satin pillow the bird had laid upon. There was a hatstand in one corner, and a broken umbrella on the floor. A line of light bled from the bottom of the door that led to the kitchen; he walked to it, said, 'Mrs Platt?' again, and opened the door.

The fridge was open, and the tap was dripping. There was a lump of cheese and a slice of half-buttered bread on a table, and an open book. He picked it up and read the cover. *Reaching the Spirits,* by Rose Daniel. He put it down and closed the fridge, and then tried to turn off the tap, but it was stuck. He put his hand to the side of a kettle that stood on the cooker; it was cold. A stale smell came from under the sink, and a scratching sound. He said, 'Hello?' Nothing. The word stumbled and died. He left the kitchen, went back to the front room, crossed it and stood at her bedroom door.

He tapped on it lightly; as he did, it swung open and he saw her. She was in bed, lying on her back, covered with a pile of blankets. He cried, 'Mrs Platt!' and ran to her; as he did, she rose up from the bed, the blankets fell down, her eyes opened and her tongue flicked out. She let out a shrill, pained cry that stopped him in his tracks. He stood in the middle of the room and opened his mouth to say something else, but nothing came out. She turned her head to look at him, but her gaze went through him. He sensed something else in the room, a living thing with no substance but grief, a ball of invisible tears that floated over her, then moved to him, then shot out of the door. She cried again, then fell back on to the bed, quivered and lay still. Now he moved towards her, bent over her and managed 'Mrs Platt...' again.

'You've come,' she said.

'Yes,' he said.

'Fred.'

'No. Frank.'

'I love you. I always loved you. Even when you were away.'

'Mrs Platt.'

'Even when you were away.'

He took her hand and cupped it in his. It was icy, and its veins were thick and blue. 'It's Frank,' he said.

'Fred?'

She turned her head and her eyes drifted from somewhere else and rested in focus. A flicker of recognition flashed across them and she said, 'Frank?'

'Yes.'

'Frank?'

'Mrs Platt...'

'Frank?'

'Yes. What happened?'

She held his gaze for a second, then turned her head away. 'You disturbed us.'

'Us?'

'I was about to go away.'

'Where?'

Now, Mrs Platt shook her head and tried to sit up. She knew where she was and where she had almost been, and she remembered how. 'My friends,' she said, as Frank moved forward and helped her. She shivered, and rubbed her arms.

'Would you like a cup of tea?'

'What?'

'Something hot? I think you need it.'

She thought for a moment, then nodded and said, 'Yes. A cup of tea would be nice. Do you know where the kitchen is?'

'Yes.'

Mrs Platt tried a smile; it arrived as a small crease on her lips. Frank didn't move. He waited for a minute, he stared at his feet, he noticed a pile of old magazines under the bed, he heard a dog barking outside, and then she said, 'Well? Are you going to stand there, or are you going to let a lady dress in private?'

'Will you be all right?'

'A cup of tea would help.'

Davis stared at the back of the bus-driver's head, and the loathing in his own head constructed a simmering ball of stuff you wouldn't want to look at. You wouldn't want to look at it or think about it, or mention it in conversation, or introduce it to a dancing partner. You wouldn't want to take it on a short mid-week break to a hotel you know in Edinburgh, where Highland dancing is performed every Tuesday, Thursday and Saturday in the lounge, and you wouldn't want to try to seduce it on a narrow sofa or couch. You wouldn't want to slide up to it in a bar and whisper, 'You remind me of someone, but I'm not sure who,' in its ear. You'd be a fool to dip your fingers in a glass of chilled wine and drip the drink on to its nipples, but it was there, it was real, and the finishing tape it would break was murder. Davis was in control, his police training had given him a strength you couldn't snap. The driver had long brown hair that curled over his collar like a wave that broke every time he changed gear. Some of the other passengers knew him by name, and talked to him as if they'd known him all their lives. Familiarity breeds grief. If you knew the bus-driver's name, he would generate your sympathy and your charity, and charity is the dominant artifice of our age. You can do without it — if you want to sympathise with someone, choose a politician, or a television personality. Choose someone who has told you that you should be sympathetic, and then look at yourself in the mirror. Pretend that Brighton is your home, forget that this is another artifice, another mirror. Forget the pretension that dreams itself into the mind of someone you have never met. Do something useful with your life. Listen to someone who has written songs that echo our days, words and melodies that are as evanescent as our lives, and as full of meaning. Forget the things you know. This is your purpose.

18

Mrs Platt sat at the kitchen table, sipped her tea and stared at Frank. She was grieving, but Joey was not the object of this grief; now she was missing the spirits she imagined had gathered around her. They were her friends, they were the ones who could lead her to some land that had not been promised, but would be plighted. Their love for her had filled her heart; as she sat, she wished she was back in bed, and that the spell had not been broken. But she had come from a different age, from a time when concern was rewarded, when politeness and manners built homes. A cup of tea had been offered, and should be accepted.

Frank had not come from Mrs Platt's age, but he had been born with an innate sense of the things that had bound it, and with a concern that betrayed the demands of his work. A vision of a cottage cheese, lettuce, tomato and pepper sandwich drifted into his head, and a hot cup of coffee.

Half a dozen clean tables, sugar in saucers, laminated menu cards, a range of fillings in china bowls, and a different special each day. The vision was growing, exercising its muscles and justifying itself in every way. He picked up the teapot and said, 'More?'

Mrs Platt smiled. 'Thank you, Frank.'

He poured. 'How're you feeling?'

'Tired.'

He put the pot down and looked at his watch. It was half-past eleven. 'Are you going to be all right tonight?'

'I think so.'

'Are you sure?'

'Frank.'

'Yes?'

'You're like an old mother hen.'

'After all you've been through, I think…'

'I've been through worse.'

'I'm sure you have,' he said, 'but that's not going to stop me worrying.' He leaned forward and touched her hand. She didn't flinch. He remembered his mother, and he remembered the way he had touched her on the last day of her life. Frank's mother had been a small woman, the sort of person people ignore, a woman whose opinion had been considered worthless. She had worked as a barmaid, a cleaner, a care assistant at an old people's home and, in her final years, as a school dinner lady. She had rarely expressed her emotions; this was a congenital trait Frank had worked hard to strangle. He struggled now. He withdrew his hand and put it on top of the teapot.

'Don't,' said Mrs Platt.

'You're more than my landlady,' he said.

She let these words float on her mind, watched them sink and said, 'Thank you.'

He finished his tea, brushed an imaginary crumb off his trousers and stood up. 'I'll be upstairs if you need me.'

'Of course,' she said, and she smiled. 'I'm not the only one in the house who needs you. Is Lisa well?'

He got a flash of the three machines, the bleeping monitor, the tubes and two nurses. 'She's fine,' he said.

'Give her my love.'

'Of course,' he said.

Davis was beginning to enjoy himself. Chips's memory was loosing its grip; it had been replaced by a sense of rage that gave him an erection. He was charged with a feeling he wanted to last for ever; the anticipation of the pleasure of revenge. The more he thought about it the more he wanted it, and the more he thought about changing his plans. He wouldn't simply take the bus-driver to some lonely spot and stick him in the throat; now he was going to keep the man for a while before killing him. He would gag and tie him and stash him in his spare room for a few days, he would explain in detail how and what he was going to do, and why. He would torture the man with the promise of his vengeance, he would teach him to be afraid. He would feed him dog food and make him drink from a bowl on the floor, and he would put a collar around his neck. He would make him perform tricks, and then he would take him to the beach and cut his throat. Davis was insane, and he loved it. It was his calling. He had been born for these days. He got off the bus at the top of Regis Road, and smiled at the driver as he stepped on to the pavement. The driver nodded and said, 'Goodnight,' in a soft, harmless voice. He was a man who enjoyed his work, who knew his regulars and gave each of them a smile. He was doing good in the world, though he would deny it. He was popular with his colleagues, and loved by his family. 'See you,' said Davis, and he walked away slowly, under the Christmas lights and the snow that spread silence over the town.

Bob lay in his bath and stared at the ceiling. He drew patterns on his chest with soapy water, and fiddled with his ears. He couldn't be clean enough. Baths, showers, saunas, washes, more showers, longer saunas. He loved water. He poured some shampoo into his hands and rubbed it into his hair. He adored the feeling of bubbles, and the thought of their deep-cleaning action. He closed his eyes and floated his arms on the water. He was happy.

What is happiness? Sadness is easier to define, so remove doubt and say that happiness is the opposite of sadness, and go home. Or stay in the bath and know that happiness is a particular collection of toiletries that come in a box that looks like a tropical beach. Peach-scented bubble foam, pineapple shampoo with a mild astringent, a range of glycerin soaps, bath pearls and a flannel or face cloth. Words, eh? They can do whatever you want. Flannel is one of those old words, like scullery. Once, Russian state censors expunged the word 'bed' from all works of fiction. Moisturiser was one of Bob's favourite words. And conditioner.

Evans lay in bed and stared at the ceiling. His wife made little bubbling noises in her sleep. He loved the sound, and he loved the ceiling. It was mottled with shadows.

Lisa lay in bed and drifted in and out of a red sleep. The hospital hummed to itself: its boilers, radiators, monitors and night-lights whispered to each other, and its patients snuffled and rustled. The night staff sat in their offices and read magazines. The smells of disinfectant and antiseptic snoozed in the air, the kitchen cockroaches scuttled without fear, and the out-patients department was quiet. All the illnesses and diseases relaxed; the night medications worked steadily, a telephone rang with a muted bell. Moonlight, refracted by a steady fall of snow, smoothed its way through uncurtained windows and glinted on neat rows of surgical instruments. Poison cupboards and empty beds, linen baskets and cold incinerators. Mice. Stainless-steel benches. Fading flowers in rank water; Lisa's sleep was disturbed by visions of these things, and by the sound of distant voices. Adrian refused to admit responsibility, her father railed and kicked the door of his cell; only Frank's voice was quiet and understanding. She had always chosen the duplicitous, the dangerous or the stupid, or combinations of the three. Like a song you loathe but can't help singing, or a film you hated but cannot forget; idiots had dogged her for too long. She was going to change her life, and surprise herself with sense.

19

At half-past nine in the morning, Evans rang Davis's doorbell and waited. He stared at his shoes, picked a cotton off his sleeve and rubbed his shoulder. He wasn't going to risk it; when there was no answer, he rang again, and put his ear to the door.

Davis stirred at the first ring, and sat up in bed at the second. He'd had a late night. After leaving the bus-driver, he'd walked to the man's house and waited for his return. It had been a long, cold wait, but worth it. Revenge had warmed him and presented him with a host of imaginative alternatives. The best of these involved stripping the driver naked and coating him in bacon fat, then putting him in a small room with eight pit bull terriers. Perfection was a rare thing, but this was perfect. Like something suggested by God, it shone and played its own music. The bell rang for the third time, and a voice called, 'Davis!'

Davis got out of bed, grabbed a dressing-gown and put it on. There was no avoiding the inevitable, and all it took was a throaty voice and a lie. 'Coming,' he croaked, and he went to the door.

Evans was shocked by his colleague's appearance; two day's growth of beard covered his face, his cheeks were pinched, his eyes were small and bloodshot, and he hugged himself around the waist.

'Come in,' said Davis.

'Thanks.'

The curtains were drawn, and the flat stank of something stale or dead. Davis hacked and said, 'Want a coffee?'

'Okay.'

'I was going to call in this morning.' He went to the kitchen and filled the kettle. 'I've had the flu. It's been terrible. Yesterday, God, I thought I was going to die…'

'Have you seen the doctor?'

'What's he going to do?' Davis came back from the kitchen. 'No. I stayed in bed and OD'd on Vitamin C. Not that it made much difference. I still feel like shit.'

'You look like it,' said Evans.

Davis tried to smile, but his face refused to bend. He went back to the kitchen, and made the coffee. Evans went to the window and opened the curtains, then sat down on a threadbare sofa. There was something about his colleague that disturbed everything he knew about the man and nagged his policeman's instinct. 'How's Chips?' he called.

Davis dropped a mug. As it smashed, he yelled, 'Shit!'

'What happened?'

'He's asleep.' Davis kicked the mess into a corner. 'He hasn't been feeling too good either. Sympathetic flu, I think.' he said, and he coughed dramatically.

'I'm sorry.'

Davis took a deep breath and made another coffee, then carried them to the sitting-room. 'There you go,' he said, and he slumped down opposite his boss.

'You sure you don't want a doctor? I could ask Warnes to call.'

'Warnes couldn't stick a plaster.'

'You'll need a chit…'

'I know.'

'So you can—'

'Look!' Now Davis confirmed Evans's suspicions. His voice lost the gravel, his eyes looked fit, and his body tensed. 'I can sort it!'

'Hey! I was worried, that's all.'

'Save it.'

'If you say so.'

'I do.'

135

The two men sipped their coffee. It was disgusting. Evans waited for a minute, then said, 'When are you going to be back? The Austin case isn't going away.'

'Give us a few more days.'

'Okay.'

'I don't like being below par when I'm on the job.' The cracked voice had returned. 'You know that.' He coughed.

'Right.' Evans put his coffee mug on the floor and stood up. 'And you're sure about Warnes?'

'Sure.'

Evans went to the door. 'Is there anything you need? Bread? Milk?'

'No.'

'I'll call and see how you're—'

'Hey!' Davis put his hand up, the mask slipped for a second, but he grabbed it and slapped it back on. 'Thanks. No…'

'Okay then.' Evans opened the door, said, 'See you in a couple of days…' and left Davis alone.

Lisa lay on her side and stared out of the window. The sky was grey, the hospital car park was filling up, a sparrow sat on the sill and tapped at the glass. Ridges of snow were packed in the corners of the frame, and icicles hung above. The sound of a carol drifted from a radio in the nurses' office, but she heard nothing, nor saw anything. She felt a hole where her purpose had been, and she felt as though she had been the angel of death. She cursed her body, guilt possessed her, her skin crawled and tears streamed from her eyes. She thought about Adrian, but any accusation was swamped by her blame, her failure and fault. She wished herself to hell, she prayed for her embryo to be given her life. The sparrow tapped on the glass again, then flew off.

A nurse came and said, 'How are you feeling?'

The words hurt.

'Lisa?' The nurse put her hand on her shoulder. The touch burnt. She flinched. 'Lisa?'

Lisa turned her head and looked up at the nurse. Her face looked as though its life had been replaced by glass and paint. It was smeared on to the front of her head.

'Are you thirsty?'

Thirsty? Suddenly Lisa felt as though she was on fire, that flames were reaching up from her belly and licking the inside of her throat. She nodded, slowly at first, then quickly. The nurse reached out and took a mug of water off the bedside table and offered it. Lisa tasted it, grabbed the mug, tried to take it all at once, the nurse struggled and said, 'No, no, slowly…' The water tasted of air and bees humming and sugar and light. The nurse pulled the mug away, Lisa fell back and licked her lips. 'Take it easy,' said the nurse. 'I'll be back in a minute.' Lisa thought about the words 'Thank you,' but she couldn't get them out. They stuck in her head. She nodded, and watched the nurse go.

As she watched, she felt a wave of rejection break over the guilt and crash against the backs of her eyes. She closed them and the tears streamed out again, running on to her nightdress and the sheets. She cried silently, she wished and wished, and all her dreams tied themselves in impossible knots, and sealed themselves with wax.

Frank called on Mrs Platt before he left the house. He knocked once, and she opened the door immediately, as if she'd been expecting him. She looked bright and cheerful, and talked as though the events of the previous night had never happened. She offered Frank a fresh cup of coffee, but he said he had a busy day. 'Never mind,' she said.

'Maybe this evening,' he said.

Mrs Platt's face froze for a second, then the brightness returned and she smiled. 'Maybe this evening,' she agreed, and he left.

As he drove to work, he took a detour and passed the hospital. He stopped in the street opposite, and looked up at the first floor, and the window he knew Lisa could look through. He sat for five minutes and wished his love to her, then he drove

on and arrived at the office to find Bob outside, talking to a
man in a blue overcoat. He parked, and as he was locking his
car, Bob waved and shouted down the street. 'Frank!' He said
something to the other man, and hurried over. 'Frank…' The
other man followed. 'This is Steve Howard, from Berry's.'

'Berry's?'

'The estate agents.'

'Oh,' said Frank.

'Steve; this is my partner, Frank.'

'Ex-partner,' said Frank, quickly.

Steve Howard stepped forward, offered his hand and said,
'Hi.' He was young, keen and had soft skin. He looked Frank
straight in the eye and said, 'Will the fact that you're ex-partners
affect the sale?'

Frank looked at Bob and the two men shrugged. 'No.'

'Good.' He gestured at the office door and said, 'Shall we?'

The three men toured the office slowly. Howard carried a
clipboard and tape. He asked Bob to hold one end while he
measured, and asked questions about the structure of the building and the piped services. He noted quickly and neatly, and
reacted to Bob's answers as though his life depended on them.
He nodded and smiled encouragingly, and moved carefully.

Bob was enjoying himself; as he passed through each room
he let go of it, relegating it to a place he did not regret. God,
he had even given up smoking, and it had been no trouble at
all. One day he'd been on thirty a day, now he was breathing
fresh air for the first time in decades. He glowed inside and
out. Health was the greatest gift, the future was bigger than
anything. He smiled at Frank, but Frank was lost in thought.

Frank remembered the first day he had seen the offices, and
how, for the first time in years, he had seen the future as ordered
and neat. Now he was being thrown sideways, and though he
wanted it, he was afraid. He had grown used to the security the
agency provided, he had thought his days of uncertainty were
over. No more gutting haddock in Ostend, forget the gravelled
paths of the Tuileries, no more putting his last fiver on Toby,

a three-legged spaniel from Betws-y-coed. Forget chaos and embrace order. Thank Bob and work diligently. Enjoy Brighton. Make new friends.

'Of course,' said Howard, 'as you know, the market's still depressed, but business premises are less affected than domestic properties.' He gestured around the office, and smiled winningly. 'I don't think we'll have any trouble moving this at all.'

'Excellent,' said Bob.

'I'd advise a sensible price, but not too sensible.'

'Meaning?'

Howard shrugged. 'Somewhere between fifty and sixty thousand. I'd put it on at fifty-nine, nine hundred and see what happens.'

Bob turned to Frank, who stared back, and then nodded. 'Do it,' he said.

'Do it,' Bob said to Howard.

'It's done,' said Howard, and the men shook hands.

Inspector Evans drove around the corner from Davis's flat and parked. He had a good view of the man's front door, the street and the flat sky. An old lady passed by, and two men in suits and smart topcoats. He thought about his wife, her perfect cheese soufflés, and her small collection of shoes. He thought about the Christmas-tree lights, and how he was going to do something about them today. And he was going to get some of those licky paper chains you do yourself. And some crackers. He would look out for some holly and mistletoe, and give some change to a wino. He would call in and tell the station that he was on to something that related to the Austin case, and leave it at that. He waited for half an hour, and then Davis appeared. He was whistling, he looked fit and eager, he trotted down the front steps from his place, twirled his car keys like a pistol from a cowboy's holster, stopped, looked at his car, looked at the sky and glanced over his shoulder. Evans wasn't close enough to see the details of his face, but he didn't miss a look he'd seen a few times before. Its eyes were boiling and its lips were missing. It was spawned by mayhem and fed on violence. It was controlled but manic, an ace from berserk. All the maniacs he had ever met had worn this look. Evans's alarms were ringing, his ears were burning, he waited for Davis to drive off, then he followed.

The two cars drove to the end of the street, turned left and headed down Gabriel Street. They stopped at the lights, turned right and as they approached a zebra crossing, a plumber's van cut in front of Evans and blocked his view of Davis's car. When he saw it next, it was turning left, under the railway bridge and up again, disappearing in the direction of the town centre. Evans was stopped by another set of lights; when he was moving again, he couldn't see Davis anywhere; he slowed and leaned forward, checking sidestreets as he cruised. A lorry honked, and a businessman swerved by with two fingers up, but he ignored them. 'Yeah,' he said, his eyes going left, right, forward, left, his knuckles white on the steering wheel and his shoulder giving him twinges. 'Yeah,' he hissed again, a cyclist overtook him and banged his roof with his fist and he saw Davis, fifty yards ahead, stopped in the middle of the road, signalling to turn right for the bus station. Another cyclist ripped by, he signalled right, accelerated, and shot across the path of a woman in a Volkswagen in time to see Davis turn, park, get out of the car and walk towards the buses.

A Father Christmas was sitting in the station waiting-room. He was late for work. A little girl sat between him and her mother, and said, 'Where's your reindeer?'

'Ssh,' said the mother.

'Where's Rudolf?' said the girl.

The Father Christmas looked down and smiled. He scratched his beard, his eyes twinkled and he said, 'What's your name?'

'Sandra.'

'Well, Sandra; Rudolf's fine.' He pointed outside. 'He's having some hay while they mend my sleigh.'

'Your sleigh's broken?'

'Yes. I had a busy night last night, and I was very tired, and as I was on my way home I wasn't looking where I was going, and I hit the top of a tree. One of my runners came loose, so the men who look after the buses are repairing it.'

'It's going to be ready for Christmas?'

The Father Christmas looked at his watch and said, 'It's going to be ready in half an hour.'

'Oh good,' said Sandra, and before she had a chance to ask Father Christmas why he wore a watch, her mother had taken her hand and walked her to the Lewes bus.

They passed Davis as he crossed the pull-ins and went to stand by the photo-booth. Evans watched him for ten minutes, then went into the station café and sat at a window. He rubbed a hole in the condensation, cupped a mug of coffee in his hands, and watched.

The air was cold but Davis breathed steadily, didn't stamp his feet and didn't blow into his hands. He stared at the drivers' office, he watched men come and go, he didn't move. He had reduced his life to a single wish, and his future to one moment. He had hit the essence of his pain, and loved it.

Mrs Platt prepared her day carefully. She went outside and cleared a space in the middle of the garden, then collected four bricks from the back shed and laid them to form a square in the middle of this space. She pulled a metal grill from her oven and put it on the bricks. She stood and looked at her work for ten minutes, watched the sky trundle in from the sea, listened to the sound of a flock of alarmed gulls, then nodded and went indoors to chop some kindling.

She listened to the radio while she chopped. A man was talking to a woman about touch and taboo. He asked if taboos were a defence mechanism inherited from our distant ancestors. She didn't want to commit herself to a definite answer, and though she thought the idea was an interesting one, she tended to think that it was flawed. Mrs Platt took up a hatchet, and hacked at a piece of old packing case. 'In Fiji, it's considered taboo to touch someone else's hair, in the same way as it would be taboo for me to touch your genitals.'

'I beg your pardon?' said Mrs Platt.

'Or for you to touch the nape of a Japanese girl's neck.'

'Really.' A sliver of packing case flew across the kitchen, hit the fridge door and landed in a bowl of fruit.

'And of course the nape of one's neck is not high on one's list of defensive priorities.'

'No,' said the man, 'but then again...'

'No,' said Mrs Platt, and she stood up, switched the radio off and went to make a cup of tea. 'Enough,' she said, and while she was standing by the kettle, she took a roll of silver foil from the cupboard over the sink and tore off a strip. She smoothed it down and then put it to one side. She chopped a few more pieces of kindling until the water boiled, and then she took her drink and sat down at the table. Joey sat in his jar in front of her. She leaned towards him and said, 'Hello.' He didn't move. She tapped the jar and whispered, 'Today's the day. Are you looking forward to it?' She smiled age and exhaustion, and confusion in a world that defies understanding. 'Joey? Joey?' Mrs Platt smiled and smiled, and her face grew youth.

Mrs Austin went to the police station and asked for Evans. The desk sergeant rang for him; when he got no reply, Mrs Austin said, 'There must be someone I can talk to.'

'About what, exactly, Madam?'

'Cyril Austin, and Diana.'

'Austin?'

'Yes. They're both dead.' She sniffed, deeply. 'I'm Mrs Austin. Their mother.'

The sergeant recalled the case, nodded, picked up the phone and rang another number. He took a step back, and when it was answered, turned to one side and spoke in a whisper. Then he listened for half a minute, replaced the receiver and said, 'Someone will be down to see you, Mrs Austin.'

He smiled and pointed to a row of chairs. 'If you'd like to take a seat.'

Mrs Austin nodded, switched her handbag from the crook of her right hand to the crook of the left, and said, 'Thank you.'

As she waited, she read a poster that warned of the dangers of pickpockets, and she watched a businessman present his vehicle documents. A young WPC appeared, said something to the desk sergeant, who nodded in her direction.

'Mrs Austin? I'm WPC Hobbs.' The woman was blonde, and wore studs in her ears. She offered Mrs Austin her hand. 'Let's go somewhere quiet.'

'No,' said Mrs Austin. 'I'm fine here.'

'If you're sure.'

'I am.'

'So.' Hobbs smiled kindly. 'How can we help?'

'I want to see my children's houses...'

Hobbs frowned.

'...but don't worry. I don't want to take anything; I just want to look.' Her voice was steady, but she pleaded with her eyes. 'I know you must have to be careful, you want to find all the clues; I know. But...'

Hobbs looked at her shoes and ran a finger along her lips.

'...but I have to see what they left behind.'

Hobbs nodded, looked over her shoulder and said, 'I'll see what I can do.'

Frank ate an early lunch; cottage cheese and pineapple on wholemeal, a doughnut and a cup of coffee. He read the head-lines on another man's newspaper, he listened to the man be-hind the counter talk on the telephone about Danish pastries, and then he walked to the hospital.

Lisa was sitting up. Her monitor had been switched off and wheeled away, and the drip had been removed. When he saw her he thought that she was someone else. Her face was missing a level, her arms were slack and her knees made sad bumps in the bedclothes. He went to her and said, 'Lisa?' She dipped her head, put her hands to her eyes and started crying. He sat beside her and put his arms out, but he did not touch her. She was rigid, her hair hung down and she whispered, 'Frank.'

'Hey,' he said, and now he took her hand. 'I'm here.'

She sniffed.

'Want to know what I've been doing?'

She shrugged.

'I'll tell you anyway,' he said, and he settled himself on the bed. 'I'm quitting the agency. Bob's going too, and he's going to sell the office, so maybe it's the agency that's quitting me, but whatever, I'm pleased. Yes.' He nodded and patted Lisa's hand. 'It's the start of something new.'

'Glad you think so,' said Lisa, softly.

'But I've got to think it.'

'Why?'

'Because —' Frank took a breath.

'Why?' Lisa wiped her eyes and looked up. Her skin was the colour of a netted window.

'Because I'm going to do something else.'

'That's no reason.' Her voice came from the bottom of her throat, like low pipe music drifting over the roofs of a row of freezing houses.

'I'm going to open a sandwich bar.'

'Are you?'

'Yes.'

'Good luck.'

'And you,' he said slowly, 'I want you to come and work for me.'

'I've got a job.'

'Stacking shelves? Selling nail-clippers to poodle fanciers? Lisa…'

'Frank?'

He sat back and stiffened. 'No,' he said. 'I'm sorry. I don't know what I'm talking about.' He coughed. 'Forgive me?'

She didn't reply.

'Lisa? Please?'

'Okay.'

Frank relaxed again and said, 'What about you? How do you feel?'

She shook her head and mumbled, 'Empty.'

'I'm sorry…'

She looked at him again and now a faint smile got on to her mouth. It creased her lips up, and her teeth showed. 'Remember when you promised not to say sorry?'

'I'm…'

'Watch it!'

Frank laughed. 'I'm watching,' he said, and he bent forward and kissed the top of her head.

'What did you do that for?'

'I don't know.'

'Yes you do,' she said.

'You've got me again,' he said.

'Have I?'

He nodded.

'I thought so,' she said.

'I know,' he said.

20

The afternoon dimmed quickly, and night drifted on to Brighton. It gathered around the streetlamps, the Christmas lights and the decorated shops, and it fingered collars. Ice cracked in the gutters, and old men slithered down their garden paths. Frozen girls ran from shops to bus stops, waving their hands and whistling. Snow began to fall. It came in slow clots, dropping through the twilight like down. The moon was thieved and the dark wore weeds.

Bob watched it from his sitting-room window, a glass of peppermint tea in one hand and a towel in the other. His body sang from the inside out, his skin whistled and gleamed, and his hair stood up in anticipation. Behind him, the sauna hummed its way to working temperature. When it was ready, he closed the curtains, undressed and opened the cabin door. The heat rushed him; he stepped into it, closed the door and sat down. He ladled some water on to the hot rocks; they hissed and steamed as he spread a towel on the lowest bench, laid down and closed his eyes.

The dark was complete, and the sauna's thermometer nudged ninety. Bob's pores opened, his blood raced, and he began to run with sweat. He spread his fingers and curled his toes, and felt a slow tingling in his right side. This gathered at a spot above his waist and fidgeted with muscle tissue. He rubbed it, creased his forehead, forgot it and thought about the next move.

In 1982, he had visited Skopelos, a Greek island famous for its prunes. He had stayed in a farmhouse on the side of a hill, with a view of orchards, the roofs of a whitewashed town and the sea. The sea had been bluer than blue, an ache he could not stop staring at. He sat on the terrace without a hat, and he let the sun bleach his hair. The light shimmered, the sound of bleating goats hung in a wind that wheezed, and an old lady on a bicycle sold him a jug of milk every day. At the time, he had dreamed himself into an idea of staying, but then the holiday ended. Now he dreamed the idea back. It lit the backs of his eyes, and sweetened his breath. He could smell the Aegean and taste the prunes, warm from their drying trays. The twinge nipped again but he let it. He smelt a smouldering wood fire burning on the shore, its light refecting on to the side of a beached fishing boat. The sound of singing from a bar, and mopeds going up the street. The place had creased with heat. He turned on the bench and scratched his legs.

As the day died, Mrs Platt put on a hat and coat, and wrapped a scarf around her neck. She took Joey from his jam jar, brushed his feathers, wrapped him carefully in the silver foil and carried him outside. She laid him on the pyre of kindling, charcoal and newspaper, and knelt down. She stroked the foil, rummaged in her pocket and took out a box of matches.

A breeze blew through the falling snow and disturbed the branches of the trees and bushes. It gathered itself above Mrs Platt's head, and spread its hands. It began to stroke her hair and whisper in her ear. It told her that Joey wanted to find a home in her. She smiled at the symmetry of this, and at the beauty of the night. She tipped her head and let snow fill her eyes, then she bent forward, struck a match and lit a corner of newspaper. The flame spread and the kindling began to spit and crackle. She stood up and took a step backwards.

As the flames began to grow, she sat on a bench and watched the sparks fly into the air and drift over the garden. They clouded and separated and hissed when snowflakes touched them, and some burst against the walls of the house, showering the back step with ash. Mrs Platt watched with wide eyes and rigid limbs, and as the fire began to lick around the tinfoil, she knotted her fingers and began to whistle a slow and mournful tune. This was a lament Mr Platt had taught her, the song of a sailor's wife whose husband had not returned from the sea. He had been wrecked on a shore she had never heard of, broken on rocks with names she could not pronounce, drowned in a sea she could not find in any map. No trace was ever found of him, his crew-mates or his ship; the storm had sucked them to oblivion, and oblivion would not let them go. She sung on a cliff-top in front of a fire of her husband's possessions; a pair of boots, a good shirt, a box of shells and a pack of cards. As the flames took hold, she sang that she wished to go to her husband, that he had been the flames in her life.

'Come to me.'

'I will.'

'Come now and don't delay.'

'I will not.'

'I have waited too long.'

'Wait no longer.'

As the kindling died down and the charcoal began to glow, Joey's corpse slipped into the centre of the fire and, for a few minutes, its smoke caused Mrs Platt to cough and hold a hand to her nose. Then it cleared, the foil began to glow and the body started to crumble. Its claws dissolved into its legs, and the feathers folded over the legs. Its head shrank into its neck and the internal organs fried. Its dried heart popped, all the mites that covered its skin snapped dead, and the beak glowed white. Mrs Platt took out a handkerchief and blew her nose, and then she bowed her head and closed her eyes.

'Haven't you got a home to go to?'

'No,' said Evans. 'My mum threw me out.'

'Get away.' The woman behind the counter flicked her dish-cloth at him and poured another cup of tea. 'You'll end up looking like a cup of tea,' she said.

He slapped fifty pence in front of her and said, 'Lot less trouble than what I'm doing now.'

'Yeah? So you're actually doing something? You're not just sitting here with a paper, staring out the window and picking your nose every now and again.'

'Yes and no.'

'And what does that mean?'

'What I say. Yes and no.'

'What are you? A spy?'

'Maybe.'

'I didn't think we had them any more. We're meant to be friends with Russia.'

'Old habits die hard,' said Evans.

'Pull the other one,' said the woman, and she went to change the coffee filters.

Evans had trailed Davis from the bus station to a terraced house on the other side of town. He had hopped across roads and dived into shops, he had jumped buses and hailed taxis, and now he was back at the bus station. All his suspicions were confirmed, but he had no idea what the suspicions meant. He knew they were real and he knew he was right, but he was confused, his patience was wearing thin, and he was thinking about leaving the café, walking across the pull-ins and pretending to bump into Davis by accident. It was a good idea, it had a plain neatness he liked, but then something happened to change his mind. A driver came from the staff office, waved goodnight to his mates, crossed the road and headed towards town. Davis tensed at his appearance, waited a minute, pulled up his coat collar and followed. Evans turned his head away as he walked past the café window, then downed his tea and stood up. 'Got to go!' he called to the woman behind the counter, but she didn't hear.

The bus-driver whistled as he walked, rubbing his hands against the cold and nodding to people he passed. He stopped to look in a jeweller's window. He thought about his wife, and he thought about buying her a watch for Christmas. Another driver crossed the street ahead of him and called, 'All right for some!'

'It's all right for you!' shouted the first driver, and the other one laughed.

'See you later?'

'No. I'm off home.'

'I bet you are!'

'Yeah!' he called, and he waved, left the shop window and walked on. He picked up the tune he had been whistling, curling the melody into twists it had not been made for, his hands in his pockets and his head up. His baby face was rosy and full, and his ears tingled. The snow was beautiful. Nothing worried him.

Davis trailed fifty yards behind, stopping every now and again to bend down and pretend to look at something on the pavement. His head was clear and his mind was focused. This was the practice run. He had decided on the following night for the real thing, the night before Christmas Eve, when children were losing sleep and animals lay brooding in their beds. He was going to carry a knife, handcuffs, a handkerchief and a bottle of chloroform. He would park his car on the corner opposite the Lamb and Flag.

The clarity of his thoughts had stopped amazing him; now he revelled in the sweetness of the air and a warm sensation that grew from the top of his head and spread out and down. He felt as though he was walking in a shower of light, that he was a beacon. The driver stopped to cross the road; Davis stopped to read a cinema poster. *It's a Wonderful Life* was showing at The Studio.

It's a Wonderful Life was Evans's favourite film. He stopped to read the poster and note the details in his pocket-book; then he stood on the edge of the pavement and watched Davis walk in the driver's footsteps, across the road and down the other side. The way the two men moved reminded him of dancing. One moved freely, innocently, unaware; the other glided and slunk, free in his own way, but trapped. Tension was wired between them, and it drew them together with a black grace. The falling snow strained the tension and gave it an edge a clear night would miss; Evans looked both ways and crossed the road slowly, his head down and his breathing calm.

Five minutes later, Davis stopped and watched the driver go into a pub. Then he walked to a parked car, opened the door, climbed in, waited for a minute and drove away. Evans ducked into a doorway and noted the time. Then he turned around and walked back the way he had come, back to his own car.

WPC Hobbs stood in the hall and Mrs Austin went from room to room of her son's house. She looked at photographs, ornaments, pictures and books. She spread her fingers and dragged them down walls, and she caressed cushions. When she stood in the kitchen, she leant against the sink and stared out of the window. A rotary clothes-line, a sock lying in the snow, a bare tree. An empty net that used to contain peanuts for the birds blew in the wind like a light tropical fruit, and a piece of wool streamed from a rose bush. She recalled sitting in a deckchair in this garden, and she had talked to her daughter-in-law about children. She remembered Cyril coming home late from the office, and she'd overheard a row. She remembered offering to do the washing up and being told to put her feet up in front of the television, and she remembered the programme she had watched. She picked up a saucepan scrubber, crushed it in her fist and bent her head. As she stood, Hobbs appeared behind her, hesitated, then put a hand on her shoulder. 'Okay there?'

Mrs Austin sniffed and nodded, but couldn't say anything. Her voice was trapped. She tried to recall the exact sound of her children's voices, but they were trapped too, shouting behind sheets of plate-glass. She could see their lips move, she could see their arms wave, and she could remember the sorts of things they used to say, but then her memories stopped. They stood on a deserted plain and stared at desolation. Broken stones, cracked trees, clouds of rubbish and dust.

'Mrs Austin?'

Trapped.

'Hello?'

It's snowing in a warm place, it's snowing in hell.

'We've got to go.' Hobbs coughed. 'If you want to see your daughter's house. It's getting late and…'

'Tomorrow.'

'I'm sorry?'

'We'll see Diana's house tomorrow.' Mrs Austin swung around, and now she was clear in her head. The police-woman tried to smile, but she failed. The police were failing. They thought that Cyril, Diana and Sandie had died in bizarre circumstances, that it wasn't all a terrible mistake. Mrs Austin knew what had happened, her heart told her so. It spoke to her softly, and it persuaded. Life wasn't meant to be like this, but it was, and there was nothing anyone could do about it.

Mrs Platt unwrapped the foil and tipped Joey's cremated remains into a bowl. She sat down and looked at them. She put her ear to them. She touched them. They were warm and grey. They smelt of spices and snow. She put her fingers to her lips, and licked them. 'I love you,' she said.

She lit a candle. Her shadow spread across the far wall and on to the ceiling. Her silhouetted head hung over her, and her thoughts held themselves in devotion.

She took a spoon and began to eat Joey's ashes. She became her bird's grave, and as she did, she believed that her own body was entombing itself. She swallowed without thinking about the act. She dwelt on the meaning. The earth gives and when she takes, she keeps. I defy you by robbing you of this corpse. I offer this bird a home you could never provide. I become the thief you are. Mrs Platt smiled. She felt very well.

Two floors above her, Frank sat in his flat with a bottle of Volvic on his knee, and he watched the television. The chairman of the Conservative Family Campaign was arguing with a Labour councillor. A studio audience sat quietly and respectfully as he said, 'Putting girls into council flats and providing taxpayer-funded childcare is a policy from hell.' His sentiments were echoed by film of the Party's October conference, and the Social Security Secretary's speech. 'I've got a little list... (of) young ladies who get pregnant just to jump the housing list.' (Thunderous applause.) The Labour councillor laughed, and then she pointed at the Conservative and said, 'Policy from hell? You should know all about them.'

'I do,' said the Conservative, 'and they're all yours.'

'Eighty per cent increase in water bills since privatisation, VAT on domestic fuel, a collapsing NHS—'

'The NHS is not collapsing.'

'Last year,' said the Labour councillor, 'and I'm quoting your figures here, there was a fifteen and a half per cent increase in the number of administrative and clerical staff employed by the NHS; at the same time there was a four point eight per cent drop in the numbers of midwives and nurses employed by the Service.'

'You can't have it both ways,' said the Conservative, and his little chin shone.

'The people want health care! They don't give a monkey's about the way it comes, whether it's one way, the other, or both.' Her voice rose solidly, and people in the studio audience murmured their agreement. Frank sipped some water, and then he switched channels.

A woman wearing sunglasses was walking down a street. It was night. She turned to the camera and said, 'This…' and she spread her arms, 'is where the action is. From the Moon Walk and Jackson Square to Bourbon Street. Buskers, winos, whores and artists; bankers, wankers and priests. The French Quarter is the Big Easy's melting pot, where everyone comes together for a good time.' The woman stopped walking and leant forward. 'Or sometimes not such a good time. In a dangerous country this is one of the most dangerous cities. Keep one hand on your wallet and the other on your heart.'

'Sure,' said Frank, and he stood up and snapped the television off. He went to the window and stared down at the street. Life was the most confusing thing. He never wished it away, but sometimes he wished some peace from it.

Mrs Platt lit all the candles she owned, and arranged them around her bedroom. She undressed, washed her face and hands, and climbed into bed. She was naked, but she was not cold.

She did not close her curtains. The snow had obscured the features of her garden; a stack of flower-pots, a rose-covered trellis arch, a birdbath. These things looked like ghosts.

Mrs Platt felt Joey's ashes in her stomach. They sat in it like lead. She listened to them. They gurgled and popped. She laid her hands on her stomach, and closed her eyes.

She saw Mr Platt. He was wearing shorts, an open-necked shirt and sandals. He walked towards her with open arms, and he said, 'How long have I waited?'

'I don't know,' said Mrs Platt. 'Tell me.'

'All my life.'

'It's been an age.'

'Not an age,' he said, 'but a long time.'

A draught blew from a crack in the window frame, and half a dozen candles guttered and went out.

'What have you been doing?' said Mrs Platt.

153

'Waiting.'

'Thank you.'

'And?'

'I ate Joey. I'm bringing him with me.'

'He's welcome.'

Mrs Platt smiled and then, as another candle blew out, she allowed her body to stop. She felt her blood slow and she felt herself drift, she felt no pain and all her sorrow died with her. She believed in what she was doing, she believed she was leaving the bad and going to the good. She would deny that she had faith, but she glowed with it. It seeped from her pores and wet the sheets, it glowed in her closed eyes and sang in her ears. She died because she wanted to, but it was not suicide, it was not a cry in the dark. It was a song to her. Its verses were slow and stately, but the chorus was up-beat. She began to hum it. It hummed to her, and the candles hummed themselves out in the bedroom on the ground floor of her house.

21

Frank woke before dawn. He got out of bed and ran a bath. He shaved. As he stared in the mirror, he willed himself a fresh face. His eyes sparkled, his lips were moist but not wet, and his cheeks shone. He ran his fingers through his hair. He turned off the taps and climbed into the bath.

The water was hot. He washed carefully. He shampooed his hair twice and rinsed with lukewarm water, and he scraped his feet with a pumice stone. He lay back, rested his head and stared at the condensation on the ceiling. He put his knees to his chin and rubbed an old scar. He noticed an unpainted bit on the wall, listened to the boiler, and read the back of a bottle of disinfectant.

He had an egg for breakfast, Marmite soldiers and a pot of fresh coffee. He stood to eat. He polished his shoes on his trousers. He read an old shopping list, then screwed it up and threw it in the bin. The egg was runny, and the coffee was brewed strong.

Half an hour later he left the house. The street was empty, and a faint band of dawn light was climbing up the sky. Silence hung over the town, disturbed only by the sound of his footsteps and the distant rumble of a train. A postman glided across the road ahead and a milk-float drifted to his left; the world seemed to move on polished runners, leaving nothing as it passed.

He was going to find an empty shop that would be perfect as a sandwich bar, and he was going to buy Bob a drink. A drink the size of gratitude. Gratitude with a suitcase and a plane ticket. A suitcase containing loose summerwear and towels. A plane to Zanzibar. A ticket to the opera. Frank swung his arms as he walked, and began to hum a tune.

He stopped at the shop on the corner for a paper. 'Morning, Jeff,' he said.

'You're up early, Frank.'

Frank slapped his stomach. 'I woke up and felt good,' he said.

'All right for some...'

'All right's a state of mind, Jeff.'

'Yeah?'

'Definitely.' Frank picked a paper off the counter and rummaged in his pocket. 'Think you feel good and you will. Think yourself into a corner, and before you know it you're out of the game.' He took out a handful of coins and sorted them in the palm of his hand.

'All this time,' said Jeff, 'we've had a philosopher living in the street, and no one told us. Incredible.' He clicked his tongue against the roof of his mouth. 'Amazing.'

'I'm serious.'

'And he's serious!'

'Hey!' Frank stuck his neck out, rattled the coins and flared his nostrils. 'What're you going to do today?'

'Sell a few papers, some fags, couple of tit mags.' Jeff coughed. 'The usual.'

'And you live with that?'

'Yeah.'

Frank snorted.

'What are you on, Frank?'

'I don't know,' he said, 'I'll tell you if I find out.'

'Sure,' said Jeff.

Frank tossed some coins on to the counter and turned around. 'It's a promise,' he said, and he left the shop.

Davis woke suddenly, and sat bolt upright. His head was raging, sweeping across endless vistas, diving into deep holes, leaping out again and slamming against the sky. He sat up and put his hands to his eyes. The pain was terrible. It stabbed and stabbed and would not stop. It twisted its point, it sliced ribbons from his flesh and it keened in his ears. This was his day, this was the day, this was Chips's day, and a day for anyone who never had a day. A day for a thousand frustrations.

This is a day for the boy who stands at the gate and waits for a mother who never comes, and it's a day for a woman on speed who cannot stop, who cannot stop flying into walls. It's a day for a man called Mick who put his last note on a horse that didn't show, didn't place and didn't return. Frustration is tattooed across the dark heart of a boy who only wants to spread grief in the world, for no other reason than the sight of it. He wants to see people cry and he wants to see them spread their arms in horror. He wants them bound and gagged, but he doesn't know why. His frustration binds him but he likes that, he likes that feeling. And it's a day that does not give itself a gift. It forgets itself. It does not respect itself. It does not want to talk. It is an English day in winter. It is English. It is the second-rate expecting the first and getting the third. It is roaring but it deafens itself. It wanders in the dark, and nobody hears it.

Davis got up, showered and dressed slowly and carefully. He made a light breakfast. He ate standing up. The bus-driver occupied his mind, but he didn't think about him. The bus-driver's face filled the space behind his eyes but he didn't picture him. He took a steak knife from a drawer and sharpened it. He took a vitamin pill from a jar and swallowed it. He listened to a farming programme on the radio. He wore a ring on the third finger of his right hand; he slipped it off and put it on a shelf.

At half-past eleven, a doctor came to see Lisa. He was a big man with a loud laugh, and he wore a check suit under his white coat. A pair of glasses hung around his neck, and a loosely knotted tie. One of his shoelaces was untied, and its loose ends rattled on the floor. As he walked towards Lisa's bed, he held the patient's end of his stethoscope to his mouth and said, 'Testing, testing, one, two, three.' He laughed. She rolled her eyes. 'Good morning,' he said, and he checked her notes and touched her glands.

'Is it?' she said.

'Certainly,' he said. 'Fresh and crisp, like a perfect salad.'

'Come again?'

'It's beautiful.' He pointed outside, then looked back at her. 'How do you feel?'

'Better.'

'Good.'

'But I'm hungry. When do you get breakfast round here?'

'I don't know.'

Lisa crossed her arms across her chest, and scowled down the ward.

'Want to go home?'

'Can I?'

'I don't see why not.' He smiled hugely. 'Is there someone waiting for you?'

'Yes.'

'Who?'

'My father.'

'And he's at home?'

She nodded.

He rechecked her notes, nodded and said, 'Nothing strenuous for at least a fortnight. Do you work'

'In a chemist's.'

'Not for a couple of weeks.' The doctor scribbled something on a piece of paper, and sealed it in a brown envelope. 'Give this to your GP; he'll give you a sick note.'

'Thanks.'

'You've got the stuff about counselling?'

'Yes.'

'And you know that if your old man wants a cup of tea, he has to make it himself.'

She laughed.

'And one for you.'

'He will.'

The doctor hung the notes on the bed and said, 'Hope I don't see you again.'

'Thank you, doctor.'

'My pleasure,' he said. He patted her hand and stood up. 'Anytime.'

Frank explained what he wanted, but the estate agent wasn't concentrating. He was preoccupied. His mind wandered. He sucked a pencil. His name was Maurice.

Maurice was in love with Rita, who worked in the same office. But Rita was going out with Harry, a senior partner. Maurice didn't want to jeopardise his chances of promotion, but he couldn't help his feelings. They filled his head and played with the insides of his ears.

'I don't want a big frontage, but it would be useful to have a serving hatch to the outside…'

Rita's skirt rose over her thighs as she reached up to take some paper off the top shelf. He stuck out his tongue, and its glistening end touched the corners of his mouth.

'I want room for about half a dozen tables, and stools at the counter.'

She stepped down, straightened her skirt, flicked her hair away from her face and tucked the box of paper under her arm. As she passed Maurice's desk, she left a wake of Amarige by Givenchy. Her stockings rustled. Her eyes were the colour of gravy.

'A good-sized kitchen...'

Rita wore a white blouse, buttoned to the neck.

'... and a flat above.'

She put the paper on her desk, then bent over to pick up a paperclip. Then she went to the back office to use the photocopier. She closed the door behind her, and as she did, Maurice heard her say something. His stomach snarled, and when he focused, his eyes watered.

'Have you got anything like that?' said Frank.

'Pardon?'

Frank shook his head. 'You weren't listening.'

'Sorry?'

'You didn't hear a word.'

'No.' Now Maurice rubbed his chin with embarrassment and looked away. 'I was...'

'She's not interested,' said Frank.

'What?' Maurice's eyes panicked.

'She's not even leading you on. You think she is, but she isn't. Forget her.'

'Forget who?'

'Her.' He beckoned towards the back office.

'Rita?'

'Yes. Rita.'

Maurice looked at Frank, and his denials collapsed. 'I can't. I love her.'

'What's that got to do with it?'

'Everything.'

'Everything and nothing,' said Frank. 'Love's just an excuse lust uses. It's fooling you into thinking you're on to something important, something great, but it's nothing like that.' He turned Maurice's name-plate towards him. 'It's a game, Maurice, and it ends in tears. Believe me.'

'Why? You're talking crap.'

'You think so?'

'Yeah. And if you'd ever been in love, you'd think so too.'

'Would I?'

'Love's not an excuse for anything. It blows every excuse you ever had out of the water.' Maurice wagged a finger. 'When you're in love, when everything in your life is concentrated on one person, one purpose, you live as pure a life as anyone can. You see the value of everything, you can begin to understand sense.'

'Sense?'

'Yeah. Everything makes sense. Apples grow on trees, birds fly, that sort of thing.'

'God…'

'I mean it,' said Maurice, as Rita came from the back office with a sheaf of particulars.

'I can see that.'

'It's not like that!'

'Sure…'

'I know we're going to be together.'

'Do you?'

'Yeah.'

'Okay,' said Frank, and he thought about Janet Black, and he looked at Rita. 'I'm sorry. I was wrong.' He scratched his chin. 'She's just playing hard to get.'

'You think so?'

'Hey.' Frank spread his arms. 'Trust me.'

Davis stood outside the bus-driver's house and watched the curtains. They were opened at eight. The milk was taken in at ten past. A light shone in an upstairs room for twenty minutes, then it went off and another light was turned on downstairs. It was the kitchen light. It shone through the living-room and lit up the front window.

Davis stood still, with his hands in his pockets. He was calm and his thoughts trod water. His nose was blue but he did not feel cold. His body felt like a huge shout stuck in a throat, trapped behind a ball of pain. He knew what he was going to do, he saw the inevitability of the day, but he could not stop. He was overtaken by desire and loved it. He was living for the first time. He saw the world spread out below him, and though devils came to tempt him, he turned them away. His only wish was breakfast in a warm kitchen, a newspaper propped up in front of him and the radio on.

Mrs Austin slept badly and woke late. She missed breakfast, but only wanted a cup of tea. WPC Hobbs arrived at half-past ten. The two women drove to the daughter's house in silence. The police car was warm. When they arrived, Hobbs handed the front-door key to Mrs Austin and said, 'I shouldn't do this, but I'm going to.'

'What?'

'I'm going to stay here; I'll trust you not to disturb anything.'

Mrs Austin put her hand on the other's arm. 'Thank you,' she said.

Hobbs tapped her watch. 'Forty minutes, then I'm coming in to get you.'

'You won't need to,' said Mrs Austin.

Lisa got back to her flat at midday. She sat on the bed, and looked around. Her collection of teapots was arranged on two shelves above the television, a framed photograph of Adrian stood on the window-sill, and a teeny-weeny fluffy bunny rabbit sat on the bed. She picked up the photograph and calmly smashed it against the corner of a table, then dropped it into a wastepaper-basket. Adrian stared out from behind the shattered glass, his features multiplied and distorted; 'Yeah,' she said, 'and fuck you.' She picked up the rabbit and hugged it. 'You wouldn't let me down, would you, Flopsy?' She shook Flopsy's head. 'I didn't think so,' she said.

When she looked at her ornaments, her teapots, her books and the stuff in her kitchenette, she was torn between possession and the freedom of rejection. Keep these things and slow yourself down, let them go and give yourself wings. Give yourself wings and watch your impudence bring you down. Put one place behind you and give yourself another chance. You can't run away, because you carry the world in your head. Travel narrows vision, as soon all you see is the road. Lisa closed her eyes, buried her face in the top of Flopsy's head, and began rocking backwards and forwards.

Fifteen feet below, Mrs Platt lay cold and rigid, her mouth caught in an expression of amazement. Her freezing rooms were still. The smell of candle wax had insinuated itself into her curtains, carpets and furniture.

Once, Mrs Platt's rooms had seen lively parties, tearful reunions and children's games. Birds had sung in them, and she had made love on the bed, the sofa and the kitchen table. The windows had looked on wild autumn storms, piercing winters and big summers, and every spring they had opened on the fat garden, its trees and shrubs. People had listened to music in the sitting-room, smoked cigarettes in the bathroom and eaten spaghetti in the bedroom. When Mr Platt had been alive, he had brought friends home to play cards and drink beer. Mrs Platt used to sit with her feet up and tell them to keep the noise down.

Joey's ashes settled in Mrs Platt's stomach, and hardened. There was a thump upstairs. Lisa had thrown Flopsy across her room and knocked over a lamp. She thought about Frank, and the things he had said, and she thought about Mrs Platt. She always knew what to do in a crisis.

22

Bob woke late. He was weak. He had a headache, and his side was still aching. The pain had grown; now it stretched from his waist to the middle of his chest. He lay on his back for five minutes, then swung his legs out of bed. He touched the floor with his toes, then stood up slowly. He was cold. He put on a dressing-gown, walked to the kitchen, and filled the kettle. As he waited for it to boil, he leaned against the fridge and stared out of the window.

He watched a pair of starlings fighting over a piece of bread, and saw a dog being chased out of a butcher's shop. The sound of crying babies washed the air, and car horns. He reached up to take a packet of tea from the cupboard over the sink, and as he did, a stabbing pain shot from his waist and slammed into his kidneys. He sat down and let the kettle switch itself off, and he listened to his heart. It raced. He took steady breaths, concentrating as he exhaled. He gripped his knees with his hands, and wiped his eyes.

There was a knock on the door.

'Yeah?' Bob sat up.

'Postman!'

'Leave it on the mat!'

'You've got to sign for it!'

Bob stood up and winced. He put his hand to his side and shuffled to the door. He opened it. The postman was holding a parcel; he passed a pen and said. 'Sign here, please.' The postman pointed to a space on a page of writing that drifted in and out of focus. Bob narrowed his eyes, scribbled, and took the parcel.

'You okay?' said the postman.

Bob swallowed, and a stagnant taste filled his mouth. 'Yeah. I gave up smoking a couple of days ago.' He coughed. 'It's not easy.'

'I know,' said the postman, and 'Okay.' He took the pen from Bob, said, 'Good luck,' and went on with his round. Bob watched him go, closed the door slowly, and looked at the parcel. It was his Christmas present to himself, a special bucket that kept bottles of wine cool. He put it on the table and went back to the kitchen, and boiled the kettle again.

The Super tipped in his chair and walked on to the eighteenth tee. It was a hot day, but a cool breeze took the edge off the heat and gave the golfers something to think about. He was a shot behind his partner, the Commissioner.

As he teed up, he felt a surge of adrenalin. This was a par four, an awkward dog-leg. The fairway was lined with Scots pines, and the kink in the leg was dotted with bunkers. More bunkers ringed the irritating green, its hole sitting at the foot of a cambered slope that lay at the back and to one side. A difficult hole but it was the Super's favourite. As he squared up to the ball he felt good, as he went into his back-swing he felt his body in harmony, and when he hit the ball he heard it sing. It sailed into the sky, drifted to the left, then slowed in the wind, exactly as the Super had hoped. He missed the trees, he missed the bunkers and the ball found a good lie. The pin was in sight. The Commissioner shook his head. There was a knock on the door.

'Come.'

'Sir?'

'Evans. You wanted a word?'

'Yes, sir.'

'Well?'

'It's Davis, sir.'

'You've seen him?'

'Yes.'

'And?'

'I went round to his place; he said he had the flu…'

'There's a lot of it about.'

'There is. But something wasn't right. I got a feeling…'

The Super tapped the side of his nose and winked. 'The old radar got going?'

'Yes, sir. So when I left, I waited for him. He emerged half an hour later, fit as the old proverbial…'

'Nine iron?'

'Exactly. I had a job to keep up with him.'

The Super nodded, stared at the ceiling and approached the ball for his second shot.

The Commissioner's tee-shot had landed in the trees. His second shot had landed in light rough twenty yards ahead of the Super's, who selected an iron, squared up to his ball, concentrated on the flag, concentrated on the ball, and hit it.

'There was something about his walk; there was a purpose to it I hadn't seen before. Like he was hunting something.'

The ball sailed into the bright blue sky, and appeared to hang, unsupported, unmoving, threatening the sun. The Super watched it, his club resting on his left shoulder and his head tipped to the right.

'Or someone.'

The ball's trajectory had it in line for the smallest of a pair of bunkers to the left of the green; it caught a lucky breeze as it fell, and bounced between them, hopped once, twice, then rolled on to the skirt of grass that surrounded the green itself.

'So I stayed with him most of the day.'

'And what…' said the Super, 'did he do?'

'He followed a bus-driver.'

'Name? Connection?'

Evans shrugged. 'I'm checking.'

'Do that.' The Super smiled, and approached his ball again. The Commissioner was coming up behind, a shot down on the hole, level on the round. The green sloped alarmingly, the flag fluttered, a few people came from the clubhouse and stood on the terrace to watch. This was a thirty-yard putt; the Super paced it out, crouched and noted the bumps and notches in the grass, and put his fingers to his mouth. He crouched again, stood up, steadied himself and lined up his putter.

Evans stood up.

'Any developments on Austin?'

'Sorry sir, nothing.'

'This business with Davis got anything to do with it?'

'I don't think so…'

'Sounds odd. You keep on to him.'

'Sir.'

He tapped the ball. It stuttered as it began to move, then began to roll, picking up speed as it dropped down the slope. It caught a bump, slowed, and veered to the right. As it got closer to the flag, it began to veer again, left now, then straight. The Super dipped at the knees, the Commissioner put his hand over his mouth, the people on the clubhouse terrace held their breath and the ball dropped into the hole. 'Amazing,' said the Commissioner, and he slapped the Super on the back. People were bringing drinks, and applauding. This sounded like leaves rustling in the breeze.

'Keep me informed.'

'Of course, sir.'

Mrs Austin went from room to room of her daughter's house. It seemed smaller than when she'd last seen it, colder and darker. There was a stale smell in the air, a blend of damp and cheese. She drew the collar of her coat around her neck, and took slow, small steps.

She stood at the living-room door and looked at an open newspaper, some cushions on the floor and a television. She went to the kitchen and leant on the table. She touched a lemon squeezer that was sitting there, she dipped a fingertip in some traces of juice, and licked it. Diana had always liked fruit. When she was sixteen, she had gone on a citrus diet; oranges, grapefruit, bran, satsumas and soya milk. That was the year Cyril decided to become a lawyer, or was it a doctor? Mrs Austin couldn't remember, and she cursed herself. She swore out loud in the freezing kitchen, and her breath blew into clouds that broke and twisted like dead, drifting fish. She tapped the table with her fingers, and went upstairs.

Diana's bedroom was as she'd left it; the bed was unmade, clothes were scattered around the place and shoes lay in heaps on the floor. A pile of books sat on a low table, and an open bottle of perfume stood on the window-sill. The curtains were half-closed, a picture of a chalet in the mountains hung over the door. She stood by the window and looked down at the street. Hobbs was sitting in her car, reading a magazine and smoking a cigarette.

There was an armchair at the foot of the bed; Mrs Austin stroked its back and sat down. As she did, she felt something dig into her back. She leaned forward and rummaged in the folds of material that draped over the chair, and she felt the spine of a book. She pulled it out, turned it over and opened it.

This was Diana's diary; January 1993 was printed on the first page, and then small, neat handwriting took over. She flicked to the middle of the book and read 'When Sandie left last night, I was filled with guilt, but that feeling was quickly replaced by a delicious sense of being wanted, being loved, being lusted after. Who would have believed it? Sometimes, when I think about her, I feel that I could drown in my own juices. How could I have missed what was under my nose? To think that we've both fooled ourselves all this time...' Mrs Austin snapped the book shut, closed her eyes, said a prayer, waited a moment, and then stuffed the book into her handbag. She stood up, took one last look at the bedroom, then left her daughter's house quickly.

Lisa knocked on Mrs Platt's door, and waited. When there was no reply, she bent and peered through the keyhole. She could see the back of an armchair, and the corner of a picture, and a silver ornament glinting in weak light. She knocked again, and called, 'Mrs Platt? Hello?' She balled her fist and thumped. 'Mrs Platt?' She kept this up for five minutes, then went out the front door, turned right, then left, and walked down a narrow passageway that lead to the garden. She opened the gate and stepped over the old flower-beds, and stood in the middle of the cleared patch of ground. She looked at Joey's pyre, and at the footprints in the snow. She followed them to the back door, cupped her hands over her eyes and peered through the kitchen window.

She saw the tinfoil on the table, and the candles. She saw a wineglass on the draining-board, and a bunch of faded flowers in a vase. She knocked on the window and shouted again; 'Mrs Platt? Are you in there?' She tried the door, but it was locked. She knocked again, and she thought about breaking the glass and climbing in, but then she thought about Frank, and how sometimes he came home in the afternoon. He'd tell her that she was over-reacting. Mrs Platt was probably shopping.

'She doesn't go shopping,' she said. Her voice surprised her. The words dropped out of her mouth and dissolved in the freezing air. She shivered, turned around and went back to her flat.

Frank whistled as he entered Beech and Crosby, his fourth estate agents of the day. He was carrying a sheaf of particulars. He unbuttoned his coat, sat in a comfortable chair, and Mr Crosby said, 'Been doing the rounds, sir?'

Frank frowned, then followed the man's eyes to the particulars, and the frown turned to a smile. 'Certainly have,' he said, 'but I haven't found what I want.'

'And what's that, sir?'

Frank explained.

Mr Crosby had just the place. He stood and went to a rack, pulled out a set of particulars and put them on his desk. 'Amigos,' he said.

'Amigos?' said Frank.

'That's the place.'

Amigos was in Burnthouse Alley. It had thirty covers, eight bar-seats and a kitchen. Fridges, chillers, ovens and microwaves to be sold as seen. An unoccupied two-bedroomed flat above. Stock and goodwill included in the price. 'It's a going concern. I believe the owner's retiring from the trade.'

'Why?' said Frank.

'I'd say he was seventy odd...'

'Burnthouse Alley?'

Crosby reached into his desk and took out a town plan. 'There,' he said, pointing.

'Nice,' said Frank.

'Like me to give him a call?'

Frank looked at the photograph of Amigos. 'Why not?' he said.

Evans left the station and drove to the bus station. He parked and walked, and spotted Davis by the photo-booth. He noted the time, and went to the café.

'You back again?' said the woman behind the counter.

'Yes. Cup of tea please.'

She went to his table, bent down and whispered, 'Have the Russians gone?'

'No.' He took a newspaper from his pocket and opened it.

'I'll let you know if any come in.'

'Thanks.'

The woman went to make the tea.

Evans opened his pocket-book and laid it on the table, and then he watched, read and sipped. When Davis left to go to the gents', when he bought a cup of tea, when he moved from the photo-booth to the waiting-room, when he left the waiting-room and walked the perimeter of the bus station; when he did these things, he did them at exactly the same time as he'd done them the day before. He was stalking. There was something flashy in his eyes. He was wearing a thin overcoat but he didn't shiver. He looked more confident than Evans remembered, bolder and stronger. It started to snow but he didn't head for cover. He walked slowly, pacing his way around the station, each footstep an echo of the one before, so his steps began to sound into infinity. They reached out and held their own hands, they comforted themselves in the face of madness, and they waited.

Frank and Mr Crosby went to Amigos, and Frank fell in love with the place. He loved the tall counter, and he loved the polished sneeze guards. The bowls of sandwich fillings. The neat menu cards. The five different types of bread. Covered dishes of buns and pastries. The smell of freshly brewed coffee. The friendly conversation of the customers. The chink of plates. The steam from a polished boiler. A selection of speciality teas. A line of pot-plants along the window-sill. The owner was Mr Santos, a Spaniard who shuffled out from behind the counter, shook Mr Crosby by the hand and said, 'Who have you brought today?'

'An extremely keen client.'

'You say that every time.'

'Please, ' said Crosby, 'this time, believe me.'

'Ha!'

Frank stepped forward and offered his hand. 'Afternoon,' he said. 'Nice place.'

'I think so.' The owner wiped his hands on his apron, and shook. 'Half a lifetime's work.'

'I can imagine.'

'Can you?'

'Yes.'

Santos turned away. 'Maybe you could explain to my children.' He went behind the counter, picked up a spreading knife and said, 'You know the way,' to Crosby.

'I do.'

'And don't leave any doors open.'

'Mr Santos,' said Crosby, 'would I?'

'You did last week.'

'Then please accept my apologies.'

'Sure,' said Santos, and he began to spread a slice of bread.

23

Bob spent the afternoon watching television, then he dozed for half an hour. When he woke up, it was dark outside. He felt better. His side was calm, and his heart was beating normally. He stood, closed the curtains and switched on the sauna.

It hummed as it heated up. Bob patted its side, and went to make a cup of tea. As he sat and waited for the kettle to boil, he looked at his kitchen notice-board. An unpaid telephone bill was pinned over a sheet of telephone numbers, and a television licence was tucked into one corner. Above this, peeping out from behind an Indian take-away menu was a photograph of his wife and children. He reached up and pulled it off the board, and laid it on the table.

The picture was taken in Devon, in the summer of 1987. His wife, Ann, is cradling Julia, the baby. Jo, the oldest boy, is building a sandcastle, while Keith is holding a red plastic bucket. It's a happy scene, captured a million times on a million different beaches. Leisure, happiness, sun, sand, children. A sign that reads DECKCHAIRS FOR HIRE. A curling wave and a high sun. An upturned paperback book and the remains of a picnic. It's a snapshot, it's an icon, it's all Bob's got, it's pinned up with the rest of his life. He remembered how he felt when he took the photograph, and the pain in his side flared again, and he grew sad.

He made the tea, and sat to drink with the photograph propped against a bottle of milk. In 1987, on holiday in Devon, the family had been as complete as it ever was; the return to Brighton had coincided with a backlog of work and half a dozen new cases. Bob had thrown himself at the work, and within three months, Ann was beginning to feel ignored and irrelevant, marooned in a sea of children and house. The things she had loved about Bob dissolved in the demands of the agency. He used to sit and listen to her, he used to understand her needs, he used to take her and the children on unexpected trips, he used to stand in the garden and imitate the cries of seagulls, and he used to play football with the boys. He used to do the washing up. He used to hold her because he loved her. Now he was too tired, too busy, too late or too angry. He was too everything but too nothing, and he couldn't see what was happening. Ann's frustrations were echoed by the children, and the echoes boomed around the house, but he didn't hear them. Ann told him what was happening but he didn't feel it. He was forgetting, but couldn't remember what. He was lost.

One day, he came home to find a note and an empty house. Ann had taken the children and gone to live with her sister in

Exmouth. She told him not to follow or try to contact them; she would write, and explain what she intended to do.

Bob burnt his anger by burying himself in work. Then he started to drink, and then he began to fill with remorse. Self-pity had him for a year, and then an understanding of his mistakes. He attempted a reconciliation, but it was too late. Ann had found another man. He could divorce her for adultery, or wait another six months for a two years' separation. He waited.

Now, six years later, he worked out his children's ages, and he tried to imagine them, but he couldn't. They were past him. He was a dream they vaguely remembered. He wished they could see him, he wished they could understand that he had changed, but he wouldn't force it. He'd seen too many unexpected reunions breed unexpected results. He flipped the photograph so that it lay face down on the table, and finished his tea.

Frank hummed as he climbed the stairs to his flat. He took them two at a time, rattling his keys and smiling. Lisa stood on the first landing. When he saw her, he gasped, said, 'Lisa! What are you doing here?' and ran to her.

'I was discharged.'

'Discharged?' He took her arm. 'Already?'

'I'm fine.'

'Come on.' He lowered his voice. 'You shouldn't be out here. What's the matter with your flat?'

'I was waiting for you.'

'Why?'

'It's Mrs Platt. I've been knocking on her door, but I can't get a reply.'

'Maybe she's out. Christmas shopping or something.'

'She doesn't go shopping. You know that.'

'Yeah,' said Frank, and he bent down and looked at Mrs Platt's door through the banisters. 'When did you last knock?'

'Twenty minutes ago.'

'Okay.'

Frank went down the stairs, put his ear to the door, then thumped it hard. 'Mrs Platt!' he yelled. 'Hello! Are you awake?' He looked over his shoulder. Lisa looked at him and nodded. 'Stand back,' he said, and he took four steps back. He braced his shoulder and ran at the door; it burst open with a crack, and he stood in the sitting-room.

The air was freezing and rancid. He switched on the light and walked towards the kitchen. His breath plumed into fat clouds. He said, 'Mrs Platt?' softly, and tripped over the leg of an armchair. As he fell he put out a hand and grabbed a standard lamp. The shade fell off and rolled across the floor. 'Shit...' he hissed, and he stumbled into the kitchen.

Lisa came behind him and said, 'You all right?' He nodded and moved to the table. He picked up the tinfoil, smelt its dusting of ashes, licked a finger and tasted some. 'What is it?'

'I don't know...' He felt the teapot. It was cold. He went to the sink and tried to turn off the dripping tap, but it was stuck. He looked at the candles on the table. He turned, left the kitchen and went to the bedroom.

He opened the door slowly, put his mouth to the crack and said, 'Mrs Platt? Are you in there?' He let go of the handle. It swung back and he saw the bed. This was illuminated by a dust of dim blue; he put his hand out for the light switch, but Lisa touched his shoulder and said, 'Don't.' She brushed past him and crossed the room, stood by the bed for a moment, and sat down. She put her hand to Mrs Platt's cheek and touched it. The old woman's eyes were open. She closed them. She straightened the blankets, and smoothed them down. Frank joined her, and as he stood, his blood froze, and his mind lost its grip on the day. He felt tears behind his eyes, but he couldn't cry. He started to make a tiny whining sound, like the sound of a small boy locked in an attic. Lisa turned and bowed his head on to her shoulder, and held him around the waist. Her hair smelt of disinfectant and lino floor. Wind rattled the window and blew a flurry of snow against the glass. 'Come on,' she said. 'She shouldn't be here.'

Davis followed the driver, who did something different. He stopped at a video shop and rented *Strictly Ballroom*. While he was choosing, Davis waited by a phone box, and Evans stood thirty yards back, outside a newsagent's shop.

There was a display of Christmas decorations in the shop window. There were foil bells, sparkly bunches of holly, baubles and a scatter of paper chains you glue together yourself. Evans looked up the street, looked at the decorations, looked at his watch and dived into the shop.

He pushed in front of a woman buying toffee and said, 'Quick!' He touched the woman's arm and said, 'I'm sorry.' He turned to the man behind the counter. 'Give me some of those paper chains!'

The man was angry. 'I'm serving this woman, and—'

Evans rummaged in his pocket and flashed his warrant card. 'Police,' he snapped. 'Now.'

The man squinted. 'Paper chains?' he said.

'Yes.'

'What sort?'

'The ones you glue yourself.' Evans pointed. 'In the window.'

The woman stood back and held her handbag to her chest while the man came from behind the counter. 'How many?'

'A dozen packets.'

'Okay.' He fetched them.

'How much?'

'Six pounds sixty.'

Evans put a tenner on the counter, said, 'Happy Christmas,' and rushed out of the shop in time to see Davis disappearing down the road. He stuffed the paper chains into his pockets, and hurried after him.

Lisa and Frank followed Mrs Platt's body to hospital, and stayed to answer a policeman's questions. Then they left and took a taxi back to the house.

As they drove through the snowy streets, Lisa put her head on Frank's shoulder, and held his hand. 'You're tired,' he said.

'I know.'

The taxi-driver looked in his mirror and winked. Frank scowled and said, 'Keep your eyes on the road.'

'What?' said Lisa.

'Nothing.' He squeezed her hand.

They stopped at some traffic lights. 'I didn't know her.' Lisa sniffed. 'She was really good at listening, but she never told me anything about herself.'

'Nor me.'

'Has she got any family?'

'I don't know.'

The lights changed they moved on.

Lisa sat back and stared at the Christmas lights and the busy shops. 'It's important to have family,' she said.

Frank nodded, but didn't say anything. When they arrived at the house, he paid the taxi-driver and helped Lisa out of the car. She shook him off and dashed through the cold, up the stairs and through the front door. Ray Butts could have become a taxi-driver, overweight, pale and bitter. Ray Butts could have married Janet Black and lost her to an airline pilot. Ray Butts could have lost everything in a fire, and ended up with a scarred face and no hair.

Lisa stood outside her door and waited for Frank. When he caught up with her, she said, 'I'm tired.'

'Go to bed,' he said. 'Is there anything you want?'

'No,' she said, 'not at the moment.'

'Okay,' he said, and he reached out and touched her arm.

'What are you going to do?'

He shrugged. 'I could do with a drink. I think I'll go and see Bob.'

She leaned forward and kissed his cheek.

'Sure you're going to be all right?'

'I'm fine,' she said. 'Honestly.'

Mrs Austin sat on her hotel bed and waited for a taxi. She was going home. She had her daughter's diary on her lap;

she gripped it with both hands, but could not bear to open it. The five sentences she had read in the bedroom had scorched her. Guilt, lust, juices; she could hardly think these words, let alone speak them. She had been raised to believe that sex was necessary but inconvenient, and that deviancy was bred in the minds of the weak, who in their turn, had the power to pollute others. Homosexuality was a disease that could be cured, a measles that persuaded the head that the genitals were less than the God-given instruments of procreation, but had transfigured to become agents of evil.

The bedside telephone rang; she picked it up, and a voice said, 'Mrs Austin? Your taxi's here.'

'Sorry?'

'Your taxi, for the station.'

'Oh. Thank you.'

'Shall I send someone up for your bags?'

Mrs Austin said, 'No thank you,' and put the phone down. No one was who you thought they were, and the diseases of deviancy were spread by the slightest contact. She rubbed her eyes, and felt a throbbing behind them, and a sweat of blood spreading across her forehead. 'No,' she said to the floor, and then she picked her suitcase up, and left the Atlas Hotel.

Bob lay in his sauna, and listened to his stomach. It churned and gurgled. The heat had numbed the regret and guilt of the afternoon; now he was back on track, and the future was possible.

He was an ex-smoker, he was going to cut down on his drinking, he was going to eat brown bread, he was going to start walking to the shops. He was fifty-one, and he was going bald. He was overweight, and he had never read any-thing by Charles Dickens. He sat up, reached out and ladled some water on to the rocks. As they hissed and steamed, the pain in his side erupted again, lightly at first, and then as a massive burst that shot sideways, across his chest and into his heart.

He felt as though someone had broken into his body and was punching him from the inside out. He gasped, dropped the ladle, gripped his side and turned over. He teetered on the edge of the bench, put out his other hand and flailed for a grip. His fingertips brushed a hanging towel; he grabbed it and tried to pull himself up. The towel slipped from its hook, and he fell to the floor.

As Bob lay on his back, the sauna's walls contracted, and the ceiling lowered. He felt suffocated. Lost. Alone. The pain grew; stabbing joined the punching, and forced him to spasm and arch his back. He screamed, a terrible wail that came from his feet, touched all his organs and blackened his teeth. He put the soles of his feet against the door and kicked, but the effort split his head and forced tears into his eyes. He gasped for breath, he flailed again, and hit the basket of coals. They spilt out and rolled across the floor, fizzing and spitting in the moisture. The pain dulled for a second, gathered its strength and then launched an attack that ripped him from his groin to his neck, concentrating in the heart and bursting it open. Bob writhed and bucked, then collapsed and lay still on the floor of the sauna, his body wreathed in sweat. His mouth was open, his eyes were closed, and his feet quivered. His head filled with a pale and desperate light, and his lungs blew. All his nerves played a single note. His body gripped itself and would not let go. He tumbled into himself, he grew smaller and smaller until he was a spot on the floor, and he lived in insignificance.

24

Snow fell steadily. Davis was wearing trainers, jeans, a T-shirt and a thin cotton jacket, but he was not cold. The driver was wearing a heavy topcoat, a scarf and gloves. Evans was wearing a suit and a sheepskin coat. The three men walked through the streets of Brighton like ghosts. The decorated shop windows glowed, and cars swished by. The smell of roasted chestnuts hung at one street corner, and the sound of carollers drifted across another. When the driver stopped to listen to the singing, Davis turned and pretended to look in a shop window, and Evans dived into a darkened doorway.

'Silent Night.'

As the carol was sung, the moon broke through the heavy clouds and shone through the snow. The men stood beneath it, and the thief floated with them. The thief smiled and his heart was black. The snow in the street glittered, and icicles danced along the eaves. Then the sky closed and the moon disappeared. 'Silent Night.' The driver's favourite carol. He put some change in a bucket on the pavement, and walked on.

Frank left Lisa at half-past eight. He drove to a hotel on the front, and sat in the bar to drink a whisky. The place was deserted. The barman wiped some ashtrays, and flicked a cloth at the optics. He was young, wore an ear-ring and had thick black hair, swept back from his forehead. His eyes were brown. He said, 'The quiet before the storm.'

'What?'

'The days before Christmas.'

'Oh,' said Frank, and he looked up from his drink. A decorated tree stood in the corner, and paper chains were strung across the ceiling. Some glittery bells hung over the door. 'You get busy?'

'Busy?' said the barman. 'Are you kidding? Last year, last Christmas Eve, we were wall to wall.'

'Were you?'

'Yeah.' The barman looked at Frank. 'We were.'

'Good for you.'

The barman nodded.

Frank finished his drink and said, 'Give us another.' He rummaged in his pocket. 'And have one yourself.'

The barman looked at his watch, looked at a clock on the wall and said, 'Why not?'

'It's Christmas,' said Frank.

'It is…' and the barman turned, wiped his hands on a cloth and took some clean glasses from a shelf. He put them to the light, then ran his fingers along the optics.

'Death…' said Frank.

'You what?' The barman filled the glasses and put them on the bar.

'Do you want to die?'

'Are you joking?'

'Nobody wants to, do they? Like nobody wants to get caught in the rain, or lost in a strange town…'

'Or burgled.'

'Or burgled,' said Frank. 'Exactly. No one invites a thief into their house.'

'Of course they don't.'

'How would you feel if you knew a thief was coming, but you didn't know when? Scared? Angry?'

'Pissed off,' said the barman.

'I don't think Mrs Platt was pissed off.'

'Mrs Platt?'

'My landlady.' Frank cleared his throat. 'And I don't think she was scared.' He swilled his drink around the glass, and took a gulp. 'She died. Today. When you're old, do you see it coming? Do you know what it's like?'

'Don't ask me.'

'I am. Don't you think about it?'

'What?'

'Dying.'

The barman shrugged. 'You never remember the moment before you go to sleep, do you?'

'No.'

'And unless you remember your dreams, you wouldn't know you've been asleep, would you?'

Frank looked into his glass, looked at the barman and shook his head. 'What are you talking about?'

'Dying's like going to sleep. That's all.'

'That's all?'

'Why not?'

Frank opened his mouth to explain why not, but no words came out. Clouds of desperate mourning were gathering over his head, and his eyes grew heavy. He stood up, slapped a ten-pound note on the bar, said, 'Happy Christmas,' to the barman, and left.

Davis was warm with pleasure and desire. He walked fifty yards behind the driver, but he was also at the man's shoulder. He could see the curl of his pony-tail, smell the sweat on his neck, and the dirt on his coat. He could hear his pleasant voice. 'Seventy pence, please, love.' He pinched his nose. 'Your stop, Mrs Perkins.' The light was reflecting on his cheeks, and on the teeth his older passengers admired so much.

Davis felt inside his shirt, and touched the steak knife. He ran his finger down the edge of the blade, and an electric buzz shot up his arm. 'Good boy,' he whispered. 'Stay.'

Chips had been an obedient dog. He had never run away or laid a log on the carpet. He didn't hassle for his dinner, and had never nipped his master. He had been the blameless thing in Davis's life, a reminder that life was not a parade of perverts, thieves, whores and dealers. Life could have been redeemed; now it could only be avenged. Violence breeds flowers that bloom in winter, that stink on the edge of marshes. Their roots strangle courage and their seeds blow on to arable land. Only more violence kills these flowers, only vengeance wins the prize.

At a quarter to nine, Lisa sat down and wrote, 'Dear Frank, I am going to Maidstone. I want to see my father. It's so long since we talked properly, and it's time we did. There's a lot I have to tell him, and things I've got to ask him...' She put down her pen, said, 'Like what?' to the wall, screwed up the letter and took out a fresh sheet.

The blank paper snarled at her, chided her and reflected all her failure. She knew what she wanted to say, but the words put a barrier between herself and the writing. She wanted to tell Frank that losing her baby had forced her to think about how her father would have felt as the door slammed on his cell. She had turned her back on him, she had not visited, she had not written. You clean your wounds as you make amends, and so you heal yourself. 'No,' she said, and she screwed up the blank sheet and packed a small bag instead. Then she checked that the window was closed and the electric was off, took a last look at her teapot collection and left her flat quickly.

She stood on Brighton station and stared at the tracks. A banana peel, some plastic cups, a rag and patches of dried oil. A man approached her. He had a beard, a blanket draped across his shoulder and a bulging plastic bag. He asked for some change. She didn't look up. 'I've got to get home,' he said. A tannoyed voice announced the arrival of the Maidstone train. She leaned forward and looked down the tracks as it came into view. The man shuffled sideways and said, 'I have.'

'What?' said Lisa. She turned and looked at him.

'Got to go,' he said.

'Oh,' she said, and she took out her purse and gave him fifty pence. He looked at the coin, wiped his nose with his sleeve, and smiled. His teeth were missing. She picked up her bag and took a step back. The train pulled in, slowed and stopped. She opened a door, climbed aboard and sat by the window. The beggar waited for the train to leave, and as it did he waved to Lisa, who pressed her cheek against the glass and stared past him, towards the figure of an old woman who was standing on the end of the platform. This woman was tearing pages from a diary, ripping the pages into little pieces and letting them fall on to the tracks. As the pieces fell, they mingled with flakes of snow that blew into the cover of the station roof, held their form for a second, then melted. The train accelerated and Lisa drew level with the woman, who looked up in alarm. Mrs Austin's face was ashen, and her eyes were red; the diary had been reduced to its covers. She turned, picked up a suitcase and walked away.

Davis had parked his car opposite the Lamb and Flag. He quickened his pace when he saw it, and got to within ten feet of the driver, who stopped on the edge of the pavement and waited to cross the road. As he looked both ways, Davis approached him and said, 'Got a light, mate?'

'Sorry,' said the driver, and Davis saw the man's eyes looking friendly and meaning it. 'I don't smoke.'

Evans got close enough to hear, then stopped and stood by a letter-box.

'You're sorry?' said Davis.

'Eh?' said the driver.

'You. You stand here, you stand here in your gloves and your scarf, and apologise to me.'

The driver took a step back, and narrowed his eyes. 'What are you on?'

'You've got a nerve,' said Davis.

'Have I?'

'Yeah,' said Davis, and he pulled out the steak knife. It glinted, its point twisted, its handle was warm, the driver turned, Davis lunged forward and grabbed the man's coat. Evans ran forward and yelled, 'Davis!' Davis wheeled. Evans rushed. 'Stop!' The driver stumbled back, slipped, fell, and lay in the gutter. Davis's eyes blanked, then flared, then Evans was on him. The man was strong but the man was not strong enough. He tried to wrench the knife away but his grip slipped, he slipped and put out a hand to break his fall. As he toppled, Davis toppled too, and the men fell down together.

Evans felt the knife tickle his side, and then a pain. He expected sharp and fine, edged and quick, concentrated; this was dull and wide, like a fist. It didn't move but it seemed to, it didn't throb but it filled him up and solidified. His life did not come and spread itself before him, he did not see his mother and his father or the places he had seen. He did not see his wife at home, or the faces of his children. He felt hot breath on his face, he tried to move his hands to the knife, a packet of paper chains you lick yourself fell out of his pocket, broke open and blew across the road. The driver shouted for help, his voice sounded miles away, lights flickered, dulled and faded.

Davis pulled the knife from Evans's side, and stood up. Blood dripped from its tip, and stained the snow. His old colleague's eyes were closed, his legs were quivering, and his tongue was flicking in and out. A crowd of people ran from the pub, the driver stood up and yelled, 'That's him!' Davis spun on his heels and pointed the knife, the crowd stopped where they were. A dog barked. Davis cocked his head and smiled. A police car's siren cut the air, and Evans tried to speak. He drew a breath, but that was all he could do. He opened his eyes wide. He closed them again, and as the air drained from his body, and all his blood pooled in the gutter, Davis yelled, 'Yeah! It's me!' He tipped his head back, curled his lips over his teeth and groaned, 'But it's not meant to be! It's not meant to be anything like this.' He waved the knife at the crowd. They flinched. 'Don't believe a word you hear,' he said, and then he turned the knife, pointed it at the centre of his stomach, and fell on to it. It pierced a lung, sliced his liver and stopped. He made a bubbly noise that crescendoed into his throat and spilt with a rush of blood. The crowd gasped, a woman screamed, a man fainted, and a pair of children were turned away. Davis collapsed beside Evans and lay at right angles to the other man, who was still now. 'God,' he gasped, but God didn't answer. God was not even close. The police car screeched to a halt. The snow did not stop falling. It tumbled and tumbled, and the streetlights reflected off the flakes. The sound of a radio message broke through, and another siren. 'Stand back,' said a voice, 'there's nothing to see here,' and blankets were brought to cover the bodies.

Frank turned the corner into Bob's road, and stopped. A police car was parked across the street, and beyond it, a fire-engine screamed to a stop. Another engine arrived, and an ambulance. A pall of smoke was growing in the sky, and flames were flicking out of the top-floor window of a house half-way down the road. Blue lights revolved and sirens wailed. Snow fell through the chaos, and chaos wore a wedding dress. Frank stood for half a minute, then rushed forward. A policeman stepped forward, held out his hands and said, 'Sorry sir. No further.'

'No!' Frank pushed past. 'That's my partner!' He swerved around the man and dashed down the street, his arms flailing, yelling, 'Bob! Bob!'

Firemen were dashing about, uncoiling hoses, carrying ladders, turning stop-cocks, priming pumps. One shouted as he approached, and another grabbed his arm and tried to pull him away. Frank snarled and shouted, 'Get off!' One of the windows exploded. Glass showered down, falling through the snow, a shot of flame blew out of the room, Frank slipped out of his coat and left the fireman holding it, and ran for the front door.

He pushed past a fireman with an axe, shouldered the door and ran inside. The hall was full of smoke, and the sound of splintering wood carried down from upstairs. He snatched a handkerchief from his pocket, covered his face and dashed for the stairs. The fireman with the axe came behind him and grabbed his ankles, but Frank kicked him off, and leapt forward and up. He screamed, 'Bob!' The fireman yelled, 'Get out!' and dropped his axe. It clattered down the stairs, a loud crack came from above them, and the sound of falling plaster.

Frank stood half-way up the stairs. He crouched, screamed, 'Bob!' again, and took another couple of steps. As he did, one of the fire-engines began hosing water. The jet slammed into the upstairs room, hissed on to the flames, and flooded under the door. The smoke thickened. Frank looked over his shoulder. The fireman was rubbing his face and licking blood from his mouth. 'Bastard,' he said. Frank shook his head, and climbed to the landing.

The smoke cleared for a moment, and Frank saw a picture on the wall. It was of a bowl of cherries. The bowl was blue, and it sat on a window-sill. There was a view of a summer meadow from the window, and green, spreading trees. The smoke thickened again, another hose was played on to the house. Glass splintered, and sheets of wallpaper blew alight. Frank tore at his jacket and left it lying on the floor; he waved his arms at the smoke, and kicked at the bedroom door.

It flew open. The heat blew Frank back. Flames filled the room, licked towards him, a river of water washed across the floor and on to the landing. The blue lights revolved, the noise of sirens mixed with splits and cracks and little popping explosions that went off all around him. He put his hand out and touched the wall. It scorched him. He wailed, 'Bob! Bob!' into the room, but no one called back. The sauna was a box of flames ten-foot wide, twelve-foot deep and tall. As he watched, the bedroom ceiling cracked from side to side, the tank in the loft split, and water poured down. The top of a ladder slammed against the window-sill, and a masked fireman appeared. He yelled, 'Let it go!' twisted the nozzle of a hose, and more water shot into the flames. A flaming plank of wood toppled towards Frank; he leapt to one side and shouted, 'Bob!' again, as the fireman on the stairs reached the landing. He screamed, 'Get out! There's nothing you can do!' A sweet smell cut through the burning and clotted the smoke. The fireman at the window saw Frank, he waved him away, the other fireman ran into the bedroom and tackled Frank around the waist, Frank struggled but then he stopped and allowed himself to be pulled back. The seat of the fire sizzled, a frying and a popping. 'What are you doing?' The fireman held his belt and dragged him out of the room, along the landing and on to the stairs. Streams of water were falling all around. Another fireman was standing in the hall. He yelled, 'Bernie!'

'Yeah!'

'You got him!'

'Yeah!'

'Any more inside?'

'Dunno!'

'Bob!' Frank shouted. 'He's up there!'

'Maybe one!'

'In the bedroom…'

'In the bedroom!'

The fireman in the hall ran out of the house and came back with two more men, who rushed the stairs. Frank was pulled down and outside, down the path and on to the street. A paramedic grabbed him, and shouldered him to an ambulance. He shook the man off, yelled, 'I'm okay! Okay!' and leaned against a car. He spat, wiped his face and his eyes pricked.

The three fire-engines were joined by a fourth, hoses covered the road and pavement, a crowd of sightseers had gathered, the flames melted a hole in the falling snow, and the sky began to glow. The sky looked like a disease. Radios crackled and the sirens did not stop. The jets of water arced and fell, a low rumble started to build in the air, and then a crack cut it, and the roof of Bob's house yawned. The slates moved away, the felt crumbled, the joists splintered, flames blew out. The fireman at the window turned and waved his colleagues back. He twisted his hose off, dropped it, grabbed the side of the ladder and slid down. As he did, a length of guttering dropped off the side of the house and slammed into the ladder. He landed on his feet, the ladder toppled, the guttering flopped on to the lawn, he ran to the front door and yelled, 'Out!' as the other fireman rushed from the house. 'MOVE!' screamed a megaphoned voice. 'NOW!' as the roof blew open, hung suspended for a moment and then collapsed. The chimney went with it, the firemen ran, the scene misted, and flames blurred, the snow thickened, the blue lights revolved slowly, the walls of the house glowed, people's voices slurred and Frank realised that he was watching through tears. He put his hands to his face, he put his knees to the ground, he spread his hands, he beat his forehead, he beat the ground and screamed. He tipped his head, snow settled on his face, and soot, and the tears swum, and a fireman put his hand on his shoulder. The touch burned, the human touch, the no point of anything, the no point of anything at all.

25

Brighton's houses stood like stones in fields of snow. Its streets were deserted, its lights played games in the night, and the sea washed its lonely shore. The Palace Pier creaked. The Pavilion froze. Gardens dreamed. Clocks stopped. An aeroplane droned overhead, and a ship hooted through a distant fog-bank.

Women slept on their sides, men lay on their backs and children dropped in and out of their dreams. Cats lay curled beneath radiators, and dogs chased deaf rabbits across flat and windless fields. A Christmas tree with flashing lights and a pink fairy decorated an ironmonger's window; a policeman stopped to look, then moved on.

A taxi-driver snoozed in his cab, the bus station was cast with deep shadows, and the railway tracks slid into the night. A milkman yawned and fumbled for a set of keys. The sky was clear, the snow was crisp and the moon shone brightly.

Footprints filled with fresh snow, and manhole covers steamed at their edges. Trees shivered in the freezing air, pigeons blew out their feathers and huddled together, and window-sills grew icicles that grinned in the night. A phone box shone on a street corner, and traffic lights blinked in time, hour after hour after hour.

The moon hazed blue light through Frank's curtains, settled on his bed, and spread to the floor. He was sitting in a chair by the window, lost in a daze of disbelief. He leant forward and picked up a packet of cigarettes, lit one and sat back. His fluids pulsed through the organs of his body, and listened to their songs. He was a prisoner in himself, but he had been this prisoner before, on a bad day as his boots pinched and Janet Black told him she was leaving for Bristol. His dreams of a flat on the top floor of an old house collapsed, the view of the sea dissolved. He knew Ray Butts wanted to live in Bristol, he

187

wanted to plead with Janet, he needed a voice, but as he spoke, the words clogged in his head and everything he wanted to say locked itself away, and would not come out.

He wanted to ask what she wanted, what he had to do to have her. Were the boots not enough? Did she want him to buy a motor bike? What sort of motor bike? He didn't know, and as she carried on talking, and her mouth opened and shut like a bird's, he realised that nothing he did or ever did would win her. He would never see her naked, she would never put her hands to his face and scream with delight at something he had done. Maybe money would attract her, give him a chance to show her what he was capable of, but he wasn't interested in money, never and not at all. Ray Butts liked money, Bristol was money and Minehead where the sea sweeps in over the mud-flats and the wind picks up along the front and steals children's smiles, Minehead was not money.

Janet Black left and Frank did not follow. His love drained away and left him with a cup of tea in a café and the boots of gorgeous leather in a carrier bag. He was numb for a week, angry for a month, regretful for another month and then he left for the south coast. The wind was warmer there, and he could start again.

A pipe gurgled above him, and a car door slammed in the street below. Frank was alert enough to hear, but the noises passed over him. He smoked slowly, and watched the fumes curl through the light and cloud across the ceiling. He looked at a lampshade. It hung above him like a moon, a private moon, and it moved in orbit around him. It threw a shadow that bled down the wall and touched the floor.

The phone rang.

Frank started, sat up and ran his fingers through his hair. He answered it; 'Hello?'

'Frank?'

'Lisa?'

'Yes.'

'Where are you?'

'Maidstone.'

'Are you all right?'

'Yes.' She hesitated, and caught her breath. It was cold in Maidstone. She missed the sea already. 'You?'

Frank sighed and shook his head. 'There was a fire... I don't know...' He stared at the end of his cigarette, closed his eyes and whispered, 'Bob died.'

'Oh God.'

'I can't believe it...'

Now there was silence. The static on the line faded away, the snow stopped in Brighton, and no cars moved on the streets. The last train pulled out of Maidstone station, and Lisa stood at the telephone by the ticket office. Pigeons huddled on window-sills, and bottles of milk froze on doorsteps. She looked down at her bag. It was blue, and one of the handles was broken. 'I was on the train,' she said, 'and I was thinking. Who needs me? Who really needs me? I wrote you a letter, but I threw it away.'

'Maidstone?'

'I came to see my father, I wanted to talk to him, but I realise now...'

'What?'

'I've got nothing to say.' She waited a moment, she listened to Frank as he breathed and took a drag on his cigarette. 'He never needed me,' she said. 'I like to feel needed.'

'So do I.'

'Sometimes I feel that I'm the only person in the world,' She shivered. 'I'm afraid.'

'Fear,' said Frank, 'is a germ. You catch it off other people.'

'I don't know what to do.' Lisa fumbled for a handkerchief, found one and held it to her nose. 'I feel lost.'

Maidstone is fifty miles from Brighton, but the distance dissolved into the seconds that followed, so Frank could have been standing next to Lisa, or sitting opposite her while they ate seafood in a tiny back-street restaurant. It started to snow again, and Frank stood up, carried the telephone to the window and looked down at the street. An old woman in a warm coat walked by, and a policeman with a torch stopped to look at a dustbin. A seagull fluoresced across the sky, and Frank allowed himself a smile. He cleared his throat and said, 'Lisa?'

'Yes?'

'Have you ever worked in a sandwich bar?'

'Yes,' she said, and Frank caught the word like a ball, and threw it high into the sky, so high that it touched the height of orbit and hung for a second like another moon, and this moon shone on Brighton, and all the houses in the streets of that antic town.

Peter Benson's new novel
OUT IN AUGUST 2012

David Morris lives the quiet life of a book-valuer for a London auction house, travelling every day by omnibus to his office in the Strand. When he is asked to make a trip to rural Somerset to value the library of the recently deceased Lord Buff-Orpington, the sense of trepidation he feels as he heads into the country is confirmed the moment he reaches his destination, the dark and impoverished village of Ashbrittle. These feelings turn to dread when he meets the enigmatic Professor Richard Hunt and catches a glimpse of a screaming woman he keeps prisoner in his house.

Peter Benson's new novel is a slick gothic tale in the English tradition, a murder mystery, a reflection on the works of the masters of the French Enlightenment and a tour of Edwardian England. More than this, it is a work of atmosphere and unease which creates a world of inhuman anxiety and suspense.

978-1-84688-206-7 • 250 pp. • £14.99

Also available by Peter Benson

Winner of the Encore Award, a trenchant critique of modern civilization, describing how one family's tropical heaven becomes hell.

978-1-84688-192-3
144 pp. • £8.99

Winner of the *Guardian* Fiction Prize, a lyrical portrait of the landscape of the Somerset Levels and a touching evocation of first love.

978-1-84688-191-6
160 pp. • £8.99

Winner of the Somerset Maugham Award, a novel exploring the evolution of an unlikely relationship, in a beautiful countryside setting.

978-1-84688-193-0
144 pp. • £8.99

Weaving in the dramatic events portrayed by the Bayeux Tapestry, an absorbing novel which brings to life a fascinating period of English history.

978-1-84688-194-7
240 pp. • £8.99

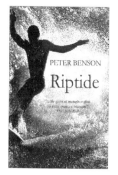

A compelling tale of surfing and coming of age, and an intense examination of a young man's struggle to establish his identity.

978-1-84688-195-4
192 pp. • £8.99

A beguiling and poignant novel about the fulfilment of dreams, the affirmation of life and finding love in unexpected places.

978-1-84688-197-8
176 pp. • £8.99